THOSE BORN IN DARKNESS
NEVER SEEK THE LIGHT

PHILIP LOPRESTI

THOSE BORN IN DARKNESS NEVER SEEK THE LIGHT
Copyright © 2022 Philip LoPresti

This is a work of fiction. Names, characters, businesses, places, events, and incidents are either the products of the author's imagination or used in a fictitious manner. Any resemblance to actual persons, living or dead, or actual events is purely coincidental.

Published by **Bad Dog Press**

Cover design by Philip LoPresti

First Printing

ISBN: 978-0-578-38813-7

ALSO BY PHILIP LOPRESTI

The Things We Bury
Where It Hurts And For How Long
Tried In Ruin

Everyone who seeks answers at the bottom of a bottle or a bag or on the edge of a knife, who keep going despite the failures, who have had to break their own moral codes just to survive another day, who hears their own ghosts calling out to them from the dark when the sleep comes slow and the worry never stops, whose scars lead back to failed love and empty bank accounts and to everyone who dreams of angels but lives with demons— **THOSE BORN IN DARKNESS** is for you.

THOSE BORN IN DARKNESS NEVER SEEK THE LIGHT

1.

How far are you willing to go to fulfill a dying person's last wish? Would you carry it with the same intensity that person had while they were alive? Would you, even in your limited power, do all you could to see it through, and to what extent is it even your obligation?

That was the quandary Finch found himself in as he was led by a black guard down a gleaming corridor and into the brightly lit visitor's room at Briar Penitentiary, where his brother sat waiting.

In a few days, Colm would be led out of his cell and strapped down to a gurney where he would ride the needle all the way into the deafening black. No one would shed a tear, except for maybe Finch himself. But at that moment, Finch looked at his brother and thought that not even he would view it as much of a loss.

Finch's cell phone hadn't rung in nearly three years, aside from the occasional call from his boss, whom he'd been working for the last two. It was Finch's first real job; one that didn't require him to travel up a drainpipe and slip through an open window into the home of an unsuspecting someone. So, when the phone rang and the call came up as unknown, he knew it wasn't going to be a phone call about electrical work. He answered it and was met with his brother's voice asking Finch to come see him. He said he needed a favor. And so, without so much as a reason why Finch packed it all up and drove the thousand miles that separated him from Fulton County. It was only now, seeing both himself and his father in the man sitting across from him, that he began questioning his quick decision to entertain his brother's request. A brooding sense of violence that Finch had never acted upon worked its way through his body like a freighter hauling explosives. He cracked his neck to alleviate some of the tension settling in his shoulders. After all, it was that exact emotion that had landed his brother in the joint to begin with. Or so he imagined.

The room was too white, and the overhead fluorescent lighting only magnified it. It bounced off the sterilized lacquered tile beneath their feet and stabbed at Finch's eyes and beyond as if trying to drive all the years of bad thinking from his head. Finch wished it worked like that. He squinted against the harshness, trying to focus on his brother, but it was just too much. It was just too white.

White is the color of death, not black, Finch thought.

Colm sat across from him with his hands outstretched on the table where they were seated. He was shackled at the wrists, the chain looped through a galvanized D-ring that was bolted to the tabletop. His knuckles were dressed in gauze, indicating to Finch that Colm had recently been in a squabble, and judging from his clean face, he knew his brother had held his own like he always had. Prison may have changed a lot in the man, but it hadn't changed that.

Colm's feet were also shackled at the ankles. He wore an orange jumpsuit—a color he wouldn't have been caught dead wearing on the outside. Finch had an inclination that his brother may have felt humiliated knowing that in less than five days, he'd go to the grave dressed in that ugly thing. He searched Colm's face for affirmation on this thought but came up empty.

Maybe more had changed than he originally thought.

Finch watched fresh blood bloom through the bandages on his brother's hands. He wanted to ask how the food was on the inside. Anything to steer the conversation from where it had been lingering and where it was headed. Around them, conversation buzzed from other visitors and inmates, none of which Finch could make out. Not that he wanted to. Places like this didn't offer much in the way of what could be considered good conversation. It was all just regret, grief, heartache, and stone-cold truths.

His brother looked better than he ever had. There was a pinkish glow to his skin, which had not been the case throughout the years leading up to the incident. His thick, wavy hair was neatly cut and parted to one side, and his facial hair was groomed to perfection. His smile was clean. Sincere. Finch tried to recall a time he'd ever seen his brother smile, but if there was, it evaded him. Even on Colm's wedding day, he hadn't seen so much as a smirk, nor the day his daughter was born. His brother was carved from stone, an appearance he'd kept up nearly his entire life. Until now. What changed specifically, Finch couldn't figure, but prison seemed to do the opposite to Colm compared to what it does to most men.

Colm and Finch were two years apart, but they could have been twins. Looking at him had always been like looking in a mirror, but not now. Colm was older, but at that moment he looked younger by about a decade. Maybe more. From the way Finch looked, you would have thought he was the one on death row. He was nearly wafer-thin, his clothes hanging from him in slewed folds like loose skin and he sat with slumped shoulders, years of burdens and family secrets becoming too heavy to bear. His brother's crime was taking more of a toll on Finch than it was on Colm. That meant something, but Finch wasn't sure what.

He remembered when they were kids and how he never got clothes of his own. Being only two years apart meant being forced to wear the clothing his brother outgrew. It was something he both hated, never wanting to admit to anyone that his parents simply didn't have the money for new clothes, and secretly liked, feeling closer to his brother for it. It was as if he was following in his footsteps, and the act of wearing a ratty t-shirt only brought him one step closer to becoming God. Looking back now, he knew the reasoning behind the hand-medowns was economical more than anything else, but when you're a kid all you think and worry about is what others might say. Finch wondered if he was still trying to follow in Colm's footsteps, and if he was, how far would he go? Would he follow him to the end and take the plunge with him?

Finch figured one of them was bound to end up in prison, but not in the way it finally went down. When you live a life of crime, prison is certainly always a threat. They were thieves. A lifestyle bestowed upon them by their father, his father, and his father before them. Born into it and from it, it ran in their blood and that blood was thick and always made itself known.

Even then, at that moment, Finch could feel it pumping through his ears.

Every thief has their thing. A signature of sorts. Some rob at gunpoint faces covered. Some scam the naïve out of their savings or inheritance money. Some use sleight of hand in card games and walk away with thick rolls of cash, a woman on each arm. Some were modest and kept a low profile, taking only what they needed. Others were all flash, using their earnings to indulge in a suave lifestyle while, inside, they tore at their own guts knowing they couldn't keep up appearances forever.

For Colm and Finch, their thing was only stealing from those who played by the same rules as they did. Thieves, drug dealers and the like. They crept through houses, bypassing heirlooms, and leaving behind jewelry and merchandise. It saved a lot of trouble in the long run. Dealing with fences would only bring heat down on them from other thieves in the network, knowing they got boosted when stolen goods went missing only to wind up in the hands of someone else. It wouldn't take much to get the fence to give up their identity, so they stuck to the shadows and crept houses at night when people were either sleeping or gone, and they only took cash. Every professional thief had caches of bills hidden somewhere, tucked away – rainy day money, retirement funds – and that's what they went for. It was easy money with little consequence. Even when other thieves had their suspicions, they wouldn't make a move. You had to be careful when you were playing the game. Spilling blood on nothing but suspicion could bring your whole world crashing down on you from every direction. No one would talk to the cops, and no one could finger them. They used it to their advantage. Call it lazy, but it was how they'd always survived.

"Hey, are you listening to me?" Colm's voice came on strong and booming, like rolling thunder overhead. It broke through Finch's thoughts and brought him back from whatever place he'd been trying to crawl into. He half expected to look up and see their father. Colm tapped on the tabletop with his knuckles and said, "I need you to listen to me. This is important."

Finch swallowed air and said, "No, I wasn't listening, actually."

"Well, eyes up here, baby brother," Colm motioned to his own eyes with two fingers. "Or did you drive all this way just to stare at the floor?"

Finch looked up and met his brother's eyes. His own eyes. Blue, rimmed with speckles of gold like their mother's eyes.

"I drove all this way because you asked me to, and I must be out of my fuckin' mind for doing so."

"Exactly, so listen. I need you to do me a favor."

Finch sat back in his chair, a half laugh brimming with sarcasm working its way up from his chest. "You said as much on the phone and I think it's pretty rich, because why else would you ask me here?"

"I don't need the third degree, baby brother. In a few days, I'm gonna pay for what I did and I'm okay with that. Far as I see it, it all comes out even in the end. Eye for an eye, you know?"

"No, I don't," Finch said. "In order for it to come out even in the end, they'd have to execute you five times."

Colm stared at Finch, his eyelids heavy as he blinked, slowly. "I did what I did and there ain't no taking it back."

"Why'd you do it in the first place?"

"We've been over this before. I was making angels, and because, well...because sometimes love turns violent. I don't expect you to understand."

"Well, good, because I don't." Finch leaned forward and felt the table's edge press against his abdomen. "What the fuck does that even mean," he said through clenched teeth, his voice barely above a whisper, but with a slight edge to it.

"Is this how you want this to play out? This could be it for us, the last time we talk, and I don't want to go over this again. I'm asking you as your brother, not as the person who everyone else thinks I am, to do me this one last favor. I'll be gone soon, and you won't ever have to deal with me again."

Finch choked up, nearly crying at the words Colm had just spoken. He fought back tears, but Colm could tell he'd hit a nerve.

"What do you need me to do?" Finch asked, knowing he was giving in. But Finch had known from the start that he was going to give in. Just being there was proof of that. When it came to Colm, he always dropped whatever he was doing to heed the call.

"There's a guy doing some time here," Colm said. "Some stupid petty shit. Anyway, he was talking, as men tend to do in here, and he mentioned a trailer where his cousin cooked meth. It's tucked away in the woods off Durham Road. Remember Dad used to take us up there to hunt squirrels when we were kids?" Finch nodded, knowing exactly the area Colm was speaking of. "Apparently," Colm continued, "A few years back, this trailer explodes and kills the three guys cooking up a batch of meth inside. Officials are called in, the bodies are hauled off, and blah, blah, blah. To make a long story short, the three guys had been stashing the drug money under the trailer in a hole they'd dug. No one knew it was there except them and this guy in here running his mouth."

Finch cut Colm off before he could continue. "And you want me to locate the trailer and dig up the money."

"Exactly. This guy in here says it's something like eighty grand. That's a nice score for very little work, I think."

"Assuming there's any truth to it."

"Okay, yes. Assuming there's any truth to it. But if it turns out to be bogus, the worst you've done is hike into the woods and spend an afternoon among nature, something you could probably use, as uptight as you seem. And if it's true, it's an easy eighty grand. Eighty grand for walking around in the woods and enjoying the autumn colors."

"What's the catch?" Finch said, scratching at the side of his face. "And don't play stupid, okay? You didn't ask me all this way so I could ride off with eighty grand just for myself."

Finch knew what he was going to say, but he wanted to hear Colm say it.

Colm eased back into his chair as far as the shackles would allow. "I want you to deliver the money to Maggie and Sarah. Take a cut for yourself of course, but they're in need of some help. This kind of money could lift them out of the hole I left them in when I was tossed in here."

"And whose fault is that?"

"Mine. I'm not denying that. I'm not trying to shift the blame on anyone else. But they're still my wife and daughter, and they're still your family too. I'm in here and you're out there, so I'm asking you to do this. If not for me, then do it for them because, ultimately, that's who it's for."

It was just like Colm to use his wife and daughter to get Finch to listen.

"If this guy is spilling beans, how do we know that someone else doesn't already have the same idea?"

"We don't."

Finch sighed, his frustration barely concealed, He ran his hands over his face and said, "How long has this guy been in here for?"

"Two, maybe three years."

"And he's just now talking about this?"

"It happens all the time. At first, you keep your mouth shut, but the longer you're in here, the easier things start to slip. It gets boring after a while, and all there really is to do is share stories and talk possibilities." Colm averted his eyes from Finch's and aimed them toward the ceiling, then shut them to block out the light. "There's an awful lot of bad shit to hate in here, but mostly I hate sleeping alone. That's when all my thoughts come and they come in overwhelming waves, baby brother. It's like they take shape and sit at the foot of my bunk, the way Dad used to stand at the foot of our beds. He always thought I was sleeping, but I knew he was there. I was always sure he was gonna kill one of us while we dreamed."

Finch heard the words and then felt them. He was free and Colm, a mad dog, was caged and about to be put down, but their lives weren't all that different when it came down to it.

Colm resumed the position of staring straight ahead and blew air from the side of his mouth. "Maggie doesn't come and see me anymore," he said, drawing circles on the tabletop with his index finger. "She writes sometimes, and I talk to her on the phone here and there, mostly about Sarah, but she says she refuses to look at me. As far as I've gathered from the few letters and phone calls, she's gonna lose the house if she can't come up with some serious dough soon. She's been struggling with the payments. If I can, I'd like to die knowing that at least they'll be alright."

"They'll never be alright, Colm. None of us will," Finch said, speaking not only of Maggie and Sarah but of himself as well. "Not in the wake of what you've done. Losing the house is the least of their troubles, especially Sarah. She's going to carry this shit with her for the rest of her life. The man she knows as her father is a fuckin' murderer. One of his victims was no older than she was at the time of the incident. I mean, do you have any idea the magnitude of the mess you left us to wallow in?"

Finch pushed himself from the table and got to his feet, his chair nearly tipping over from the force at which he stood up. It let out a grating noise like nails on a chalkboard as the legs slid along the tile floor. The other voices in the room came to a halt, all eyes suddenly on Finch and Colm. Finch looked around at the corners of the room and spotted the guard who had escorted him in. He stood with another uniformed man. They talked over their shoulders at one another. Finch threw up his hand to get his attention and to signal he was done with the visit.

"I'll do what you're asking." Finch looked down at Colm, a handsome man driven to do a terrible thing that he would never explain. "But know this: I'm not doing it for you. I'm not even doing it for Maggie. I'm doing it for Sarah. And if this works out, I'm going to suggest that Maggie use the money to get her and Sarah as far away from here as possible and change their last name, putting you in the ground and behind them once and for all." Finch put his palms flat on the table, leaned into Colm, and kissed him on the forehead. With a tremble in his voice, he whispered, "You're my brother, Colm, and I love you, but I fuckin' hate you in equal measure and I don't feel the least bit bad about it. My only regret is that when you die and I cry over your passing, the tears won't be for someone more deserving."

Colm sat silent.

The guard approached and began unshackling him from the D-ring. Finch turned and weaved through the visitor's tables. He was gone before Colm was out of his chair.

2.

Sheriff Lou Rawlins sat in the parked cruiser in a pull-off along the only stretch of paved road in Fulton County. He uncapped a thermos and poured hot coffee into the lid that doubled as a cup. He sipped at it a couple of times before adding a bit of bourbon to it from the flask he kept in the glove compartment. He shifted in his seat and adjusted his gun belt. His gut was starting to extend over it and so he loosened it a notch. He didn't know when that happened, but he was getting older, and the weight seemed to be following.

Rawlins placed the cup on the dashboard and lit a cigarette, rolling down the driver's side window to blow streams of smoke out into the cool autumn air. He could smell the rain as he closed his eyes and took in the silence with pleasure, grateful for small moments like this. He rubbed at his aching knee, the result of a childhood incident involving him taking an aluminum baseball bat to the kneecap and shattering it, culminating in a forever limp that got especially bad when the weather was damp.

When he opened his eyes to retrieve the cup from the dashboard, he caught a glimpse of himself in the rearview mirror. His once thick head of hair was now thin and wispy, having started to go to seed. His eyes seemed to be receding, sunk too far back into his skull, and his pockmarked face was now bloated from too much alcohol. He wasn't much of a looker, and he knew it. It was one of the reasons he was pushing fifty and still single. He was a man with a weathervane personality and a hair-trigger temper. Being sheriff of a small town didn't get you points with the locals—especially when becoming sheriff of a small town didn't take much more than showing up. Being hated came with the territory, so rather than play devil's advocate, he just played the devil.

A light rain began to speck the windshield as he finished his cigarette. When he was done, he tossed it to the road outside and watched embers from the cherry dance across the asphalt, motivated by a passing breeze that kicked up dead leaves and brushed them up against the cruiser. He finished the rest of the coffee in his cup with one sip, re-screwed the lid back on, and was placing it on the passenger seat when the dispatch radio crackled. The voice of dispatcher Pam Tibbins came through, telling him of a house fire not two miles from where he sat.

"Lou, I think Tucker Fodee and BoDeen Carlson finally gone and set themselves ablaze," she said. "Tucker sounded pretty frantic."

"What's he calling us for? He should be calling the fire department."

"I don't know. He actually wanted your personal number, but I wouldn't give it up."

"For what?"

"Didn't say." There was silence for a moment before Pam said, "Lou?"

"Yes?" he responded, a slight annoyance evident in his voice, knowing that his quiet night would now be spent cleaning up a mess.

"I think he has the baby with him."

"Oh, for Christ's sake. I'm on my way."

Rawlins pulled onto the shoulder of the road and leaned his head out the window. He spat through his teeth before gunning it down the hot burn of razor black, the siren blaring to life and throwing colors of blue and red against the tree lines. Once he hit seventy miles per hour, he maintained the speed until he reached the turnoff.

By the time he reached the house, which was located down a thin cut of gravel, fire had already consumed most of the guts and the frame was collapsing in on itself. He parked the cruiser on the lawn and noticed Tucker kneeling out front, his head in his hands. The left sleeve of his green army jacket was blackened where flames had crawled up his arm but were extinguished by the time it reached his shoulder. The faint sound of sirens sounded off from the same direction Rawlins had arrived as he approached Tucker.

Someone called it in, Rawlins thought, *Probably Pam.*

When Rawlins reached Tucker's slumped form on the brown lawn, he saw he was kneeling at the body of BoDeen Carlson, Tucker's friend and partner in crime. BoDeen was lying on his back, legs and arms spread out like he was making snow angels. A closer look revealed that he'd been caught in the flames. His clothes were melted to his skin, to the point you couldn't tell where they ended, and his actual skin began. The few parts you could see were now charcoaled jelly, nearly sliding off his hands, face, and neck in waxy drips. His lips were gone, as were his eyebrows. Rawlins almost tossed his dinner in the yard after getting a look at BoDeen's face, now a lump of wet bubblegum.

"Well, you finally went and did it, Tuck."

"I told him to wait. I told him not to do anything until I got back."

"Where's the baby, Tuck?"

"I don't know what he was thinking," Tucker continued, ignoring the question.

"The baby," Rawlins repeated, placing his hands on Tucker's shoulders. "Where is he?"

A series of nuanced tremors worked themselves through Tucker's body, settled in, and took over. Rawlins watched as the realization of what was happening took hold of the twenty-five-year-old kid who knelt at his feet. His body shook uncontrollably with slight bursts of movement. "He's in the truck," Tucker said, the shaking working its way into his voice.

"Why the hell did you bring a baby to a cookout?" Rawlins threw a glance over his shoulder at the brown Bronco parked ten feet behind them.

"Darlene had to work. I didn't have much of a choice."

"We always have choices; you just didn't like the ones you had," Rawlins said. "Or you couldn't speak up. Or both."

"What the fuck does that mean?" Tucker rubbed at his nose with his burnt sleeve, leaving a smudge of black across his face, and looked over at Rawlins, who was walking away.

"It means put your foot down. Tell that floozy to stop slinging her ass all over town and stay home and take care of her kid," Rawlins spoke the words toward the sky as he made his way over to the Bronco. He cupped his hands to frame his eyes and peered into the passenger side window. A reflection of flames, like a serpent's tongue, licked upward, nearly obscuring his view of the interior. Inside, on the passenger seat, lay the baby, wrapped in a sweatshirt that was streaked with oil stains. He bucked his legs and cooed gibberish, a slight smile across his face as he shook the rattle Tucker had given him.

Tucker didn't have a response to what Rawlins had said. He wavered on his knees, a gas mask still clutched in his hand, eyes screwed shut while his lips moved. No sound came though. It looked like he was trying to wish away the whole situation through quiet prayer.

"Why the fuck did you call the office asking for me and my number?" Rawlins asked, retracing his steps to reclaim his spot next to Tucker. "You know what kind of shit that could bring down on this whole operation. I told you, no phones. Stupid move, Tuck." He spit through his teeth. "And why don't you have my number anyway?"

"New phone." Tucker reached into his pocket to reveal a prepaid cell phone, blue in color and waved it in Rawlins' direction. "Had to get rid of the other one. And I panicked, okay. I didn't know what else to do."

"You fuckin' call 911 and ask for the fire department. You leave him inside and take off. Hell, you try to put the flames out with your own fuckin' piss, I don't care. Anything but call asking for me and my personal number. I have Pam dispatching me and mentioning yours and BoDeen's name. She mentioned the baby. Did you tell her he was here with you?"

"I might have mentioned it. I was frantic, I don't remember."

"Well, you did. For fuck's sake, Tuck. It's this kind of shit that's gonna bring this whole situation to a head. I don't need Pam asking questions. Everyone already knows what you and BoDeen are up to, and they wonder why I can't seem to haul you in. We don't need any more suspicion." Rawlins hung his head and pinched the bridge of his nose. "Did you at least save some of the works?"

Tucker hesitated for a moment, then swallowed and said, "No, it all went up with the house."

"You dipshit. You took a fuckin' IQ test and it came back negative. You truly are a five-star fuck up, you know that?"

Tucker did his best to let the words roll off his back, but comments like that always cut right through him. He roughed it out and didn't let Rawlins know that it bothered him, but only because there were bigger, more pressing things to worry about at the moment.

"I told you, I asked BoDeen to wait for me to get back. I came out here to check on Tobias and bring out the first batch. I was gonna head back in and finish mixing up what was already started and grab the second batch and schlep it out here to the truck. No sooner do I turn around, I'm tossed to the grass and it's raining fuckin' splinters and flames on my head and my ears are ringing."

"How you gonna pay up at the end of the month now?"

"Is that all you care about?"

"Are you fuckin' kiddin' me?" Rawlins waited for an answer but got nothing. "News flash, yes, that is all I care about. What else would I care about? You? Him?" Rawlins pointed to BoDeen, sprawled out on the lawn. "You think I'm in the business to look after the wellbeing of two go nowhere losers? You pay me to look the other way and to haul in any competition. That's how this works. It's how it's worked from the beginning. There's no other reason for me to be involved other than to take a cut and ensure you don't go to prison. Without that tradeoff you're just another criminal. I should end it now and cuff your ass."

"You'll get your money," Tucker spoke the words through clenched teeth.

"Oh, I know I will. That much is a guarantee."

"I don't like the situation any more than you do. You think I like owing a debt to you every month, sucking up my funds? Because I don't, Lou. You didn't give me much of a choice in the matter. I could have gone my whole life without you finding out what I was up to, but that's not how the road bent, and neither one of us can make it bend the other way. We're already on it and we have no choice but to ride it to the end."

Rawlins puffed out his chest like he was ready to go head-to-head with Tucker, rage idling through him, but the feeling was cut short as a low sound escaped BoDeen's throat. It sounded like someone was blowing bubbles through a straw into a glass of milk. He was trying to form words, but the heat had singed his vocal cords and throat. He was only able to gurgle and sputter, sounding almost like a baby. Tucker and Rawlins fixed their gaze on BoDeen. A light wind blew, wafting the smell of BoDeen's cooked body into their faces. It reminded Lou of overcooked venison.

"Fuck, he's still alive." Tucker looked over his shoulder at Rawlins.

The sheriff's eyes were like two black stones tossed in dirt.

"I'm not sure what you call that, but 'alive' is not it," Rawlins said and removed a handkerchief from his back pocket. He dabbed at the sweat on his face caused by the heat coming off the burning house then held it to his nose to stave off the smell of BoDeen. His shoulders fell into a slump as he turned away to face the cooler air at his back.

He sighed, "Shit," as he listened to BoDeen struggle to form words.

"We have to do something." Tucker stood and began to pace, trying to look away from the burnt mess of his friend, but finding it nearly impossible to keep his gaze anywhere else.

Rawlins removed the handkerchief from his face. "Not much we can do," he said and wiped at the edges of his mouth with a forefinger and thumb. "He won't survive this and even if he could, he wouldn't want to."

"Well, we can't let him suffer like this."

"Goddammit," Rawlins said, knowing Tucker wasn't capable of doing what needed to be done.

Rawlins approached BoDeen's body and looked down at what used to be his face, at his eyes rimmed with charred skin. "Sorry, kid," he said. He placed a boot on his neck and jammed all his weight onto his windpipe. BoDeen's eyelids peeled themselves from his face as his eyes went wide, looking into the face of the man that was going to kill him. There was a loud cracking noise, followed by a pop, and then BoDeen was dead as he'd ever be.

The sound of the fire engines edged closer. Tucker was bent over, turned away from the body with his hands on his knees. He hurled into the yard, a steady stream of that morning's breakfast working its way up from his stomach. It spattered at his feet below. Brown grass crunched under his work boots as he struggled to keep his balance. He turned back toward Rawlins and BoDeen's body, wiping puke from his chin. Flames continued to lick upward to the darkening sky, casting an auburn glow across the two men's faces as they stood together in stunned silence, tension working its way through both their bodies. The rain picked up, falling heavier and more steadily. It felt like pins and needles on the backs of their necks and sizzled on the flames.

"You got a tarp in that truck of yours?"

"No," Tucker said, spitting to the ground, the taste of puke still burning the inside of his mouth.

"Fuck it, I have some blankets in the back of my cruiser. We're gonna wrap his body up and put it in the bed of your truck. I'm gonna take the baby to Darlene and you're gonna drive over to the lake and wait for me."

"What are we gonna do at the lake?"

"We're gonna clean up this mess."

3.

There was only one way back to the motel; a single road that cut a swath through rough, winding hills flanked by an expanse of woodland thick with deadfall and blighted cornfields. Not a single streetlight existed through the entire stretch, as if someone intentionally didn't install them, thinking it was better if this area remained in the dark. It was the only road that connected Fulton to Greensborough, the place the prison was located. For Finch, it was a long drive to have to make when all he had was himself and the voice of his soon-to-be-dead brother twisting in his head, scraping at the inside of his skull like a hot shiv.

He turned on the radio and found a jazz station. A slow, smoky trumpet drifted from the speakers and made Finch think of all the times he and Colm would drive around and plan jobs while Maggie sat in the back seat filing her nails and snapping bubblegum. He looked in the review mirror at his reflection and for a moment, it was like looking into the past. Not only was he there in the mirror's reflection, but he could see Colm and Maggie too. She blew a bubble, popped it with an intake of air, sucked it back into her mouth and, looking at Finch in the mirror, said, "Fulton, a boring fucking place that's a long drive from other boring fuckin' places, huh, Finch?" He shut his eyes tight for a few moments, not wanting to relive old memories, especially those involving Maggie. He shut the radio off and, keeping his eyes glued to the road, drove the rest of the way in silence.

/ / /

In the time it took him to drive back to the motel, the sky had opened with a light, but steady October rain. Finch rolled down the driver's side window, reached out with his left hand, and felt the sting of it against his palm. The darkness opened wide through the windshield of his '62 ragtop Impala, only barely kept at bay by the headlights and the ever-present moon overhead that spilled its milky neon across the wet street like busted candy.

The Impala had been the car of his father's youth. Finch had heard the stories—most of them more than once—about his father's lead-footed shenanigans involving outrunning local cops over minor offenses and enraged neighbors awakened at two in the morning to the sound of his father opening the engine to gun it down their suburban street, leaving a trail of smoke in his wake. It did little other than annoy them and even though he kept the car well past middle age, it didn't help him hold on to the confidence and excitement one seems to be filled with at that age. If anything, it only served in making him a more embittered man. It was a reminder of something he once had that could never be regained, and a time when the thought of a wife and kids never crossed his mind. He had a way of acting like he was the only one age had happened to.

Even still, he treated the car better than he did his wife and kids. Finch and Colm weren't allowed anywhere near it. He searched his mind and, to the best of his recollection, could only remember a single time he and Colm had ever even ridden in the damn thing as children. It was on a Tuesday during summer break when their father came home, appearing in an overwhelmingly good mood. He walked into the kitchen where Colm and Finch's mother, Anna, was cleaning up and pulled her away from her chores, beginning to waltz with her around the kitchen. Colm and Finch side-eyed one another from their places at the kitchen table where they sat eating lunch, smirks across their faces.

"What's gotten into you?" Anna asked, a smile forming on her lips. But their father didn't answer. He just kissed her and said, "Let's all go for a drive. It's a beautiful day and I would like to spend it with my wife and children."

Colm had filched two popsicles from the freezer before their father piled them and their mother into the car and, with the windows opened wide and the summer wind whipping through the interior, they had at the cold treats. By the time it was over, half of them had melted due to the sweltering summer heat and with their fingers sticky, they left evidence all over the back seat. Later, when they returned home and their father saw the drips of sticky red left behind from their dirty hands, he took it as an act of betrayal. He spent the rest of the day cleaning up the interior, cursing under his breath, while their mother did her best to console Colm and Finch because while their father rarely raised a hand to either of them, they sure got an earful. Hiram McAllister had a tongue that could wield enough damage, spitting words of discouragement and hate that would have you questioning everything about yourself. Even at thirty-nine, Finch still heard his father's voice criticizing him. It was because of this that Finch had learned early on that the most dangerous part of a person was not their fists but their mouth.

And now the car was his, but not before it was Colm's, and the only reason he'd inherited it in the first place was because their old man finally ran his mouth to the wrong person and ended up with a screwdriver in his frontal lobe. Their mother followed a couple of years later, cancer eating away at what little was left of her. In the end, it was Finch and Colm. That is until Colm walked off down the back alleyways of his black pain, never to return, no matter how hard Finch went kicking and screaming into his sleep.

Finch did little to maintain the car. He was never into cars much, not like his old man or even Colm, and knew even less about them. He sometimes thought it was an act of defiance as if he were saying, "Fuck you." A way to say to his father now what he couldn't when the old bastard was still alive.

/ / /

The motel was left over from the 1980s. A single-story brick structure with twelve rooms or so and a giant neon sign at the foot of the parking lot that read Blue Swallow Inn. Next to the motel was a railcar-style diner called Dolly's and across the street was a gas station with only two pumps. Nothing else existed for twenty miles in either direction.

By the time Finch pulled into the motel parking lot, the storm had fully rolled in and was coming down in buckets. He killed the engine with a turn of the key and sat for a while just listening to it pound at the windshield and roof, the interior becoming a furious swoosh of white noise, like a thousand rounds of birdshot being blasted against the side of a tin shack.

He didn't want it to end. When it did, he'd be forced to confront his brother and what he'd asked him to do. Colm wasn't dead yet, but he'd haunted Finch just the same, much like he had his entire life. It was the nature of their relationship.

As far as Finch could tell, there was no one else staying at the motel. The only other car in the lot belonged to the clerk at the check-in desk. She was a young Native American woman whose smile was brilliantly white and who had spoken in a near whisper when Finch had checked in earlier that day. He made a note of it because he had to ask her to repeat nearly everything she'd said to the point that he started to wonder if it was his hearing that was going rather than the way she spoke. He thought for a few moments about going in and lying to her about needing fresh towels, just to see a friendly, unfamiliar face. Only back four hours and already he was looking for a distraction from what lay in wait.

Inside his motel room, Finch grabbed a towel from the bathroom and dried off. He'd gotten drenched in the short time it took him to make it from the car to the door. Now he stood dead center of the room, dripping all over the carpet as he worked the towel over his face and hair. When he was done, he stripped down to his boxer-briefs and lay on the bed, hoping the tension in his muscles would work itself out. The cool air of the room felt good against his damp skin and eased the burning he felt inside.

He looked at the clock on the bedside table. It was only seven. If he left now, he could make it to Maggie's by twenty after. He should make an appearance. Her husband was going to be executed in three days. He should check in on her and Sarah, he thought, before realizing he was placing too much importance on himself. He hadn't seen them in damn near three years. What did they need him for? They'd been doing fine this whole time without him. It was selfishly motivated anyway because when it came down to it, he wanted to see them for his own reasons more than he wanted to know how they were doing. He suspected they were doing just about as good as two people could, given the circumstances.

Finch rolled away from the clock, suddenly feeling more tired than he had realized. He closed his eyes and quickly found sleep, dreaming of things he had no right to. Things he hadn't dreamed of in a long time.

/ / /

He awoke a couple of hours later feeling no different than he had before drifting off. Thing was, it didn't matter if he slept four hours or four days because Finch wasn't that kind of tired. The kind of sleep Finch yearned for rarely happened this side of the grave. It had been like that nearly his entire life.

He pulled himself from the bed, went into the bathroom, pissed, swallowed three aspirin, and splashed cold water on his face without turning on the light. He got dressed in fresh, dry clothes and decided to take a ride into town. Outside the rain had stopped, but he could hear rumblings in the distance of another storm on its way. He got into the Impala, fired it up, and took a right out of the parking lot, the tailpipe coughing smoke into the damp night.

He made it to town in fifteen minutes and drove the streets for a bit, taking in the sites and old haunts. Not much had changed in three years. He didn't know if that was a good thing or bad. Most of us are reluctant to change but quick to bitch when everything stays the same, always living in that space of stagnation while quietly bursting at the seams with desperation for something more, even when we don't know what it is that we want.

He thought about picking up a streetwalker and having a go in the back seat of the Impala. It had been a while since he'd felt the touch of another. It had been even longer since he'd worked out years of rage and regret between the legs of a woman. Finch felt the burning need like a knife twisting into his side. It was still early enough that the Cat House would be open. He could find what he wanted there.

The Cat House was a low-bottom bar and strip club. One where most of the clientele was on a first name basis and would often show up half in the bag, having already drunk themselves stupid down at the trailer park. It smelled of stale cigarette smoke and cheap beer. When Finch and Colm were younger, they used to joke about how it was the kind of strip club where you throw loose change at the dancers. It was a place where time was not measured in the same terms as the outside world. Anything could happen at The Cat House, and it often did.

He pulled into the gravel parking lot and parked the Impala between two pickup trucks. Finch saw a few more scattered throughout the parking lot. The good ole boys were out tonight which meant it could get rowdy if it hadn't already. He could hear the bass from the bar thumping from the driver's seat. He watched people come and go, the giant neon sign fixed to the lip of the roof, throwing shades of candy red against their skin as they walked in and out of the joint. It was a full house tonight.

Before heading into the bar, Finch removed a .38 revolver from the glove box, opened its cylinder, and removed five bullets, leaving one tucked into its chamber. He then proceeded to give the cylinder a forceful spin as if he were spinning a roulette wheel, knowing everything that came next banked on where it landed. He threw the loose bullets into the cup holder, stuffed the revolver under the back seat, and pushed himself out into the light drizzle and across the parking and into the bar.

Inside, the music was enough to beat you into submission. He took a seat at the long, railed bar and ordered two fingers of Dewars, neat. The bartender brought him his drink and set it on a napkin he'd tossed on the bar in front of Finch. He downed it in two swigs and quickly ordered another, but this time on the rocks. He'd drink this next one slowly and then spend the rest of the night sucking on ice cubes. It was easy to kill a bottle and if Finch had learned anything in life, it was that the bottom of a bottle came quick but could easily seem just as endless when you were pouring out your heart.

At Finch's back, in the center of the room, was a circular stage with a thin catwalk that led to the back of the bar where women would appear from behind a curtain and do their thing. He spun in his chair to face the magic and sipped at his drink.

The stage was outlined with a string of Christmas lights and the woman at its center had been introduced as Belladonna. She was slender and pale, with large breasts that had a natural sag to them and a head full of wild, fiery red hair. Men crowded the front of the stage waving money, hootin' and hollerin' as she worked the pole in sync with the music before slowly peeling off a purple top, revealing the goods. Beyond them, a mixed audience of men and women, some single, some of them couples, leaned into one another, trying to converse over the music. A few stragglers crowded the corner, playing pool. It seemed to be getting heated between two men, a good chunk of money no doubt riding on the game.

Finch traced the interior of the bar with his eyes looking out for a working girl, but most of them seemed to be busy already working on closing a deal. It was a smart move on their part. Wait for the men to get full of liquor and, egged on by a few lap dances, go in for the kill when they could no longer take it and were just about ready to pop. It was guaranteed money. It wasn't unlike Finch and Colm, waiting for others to do all the work and then slipping into a dark house, emerging with the goods.

At the front of the bar were two large windows that overlooked the parking lot. They had been painted over in a thick black, dry drip marks visibly running down the glass to keep those passing from getting a free show and to keep Christian types from picketing the abhorrent behavior that was ruining the minds of their children.

"Wanna buy a lady a drink?" A voice cut through the noise that filled the bar.

Finch called the bartender over. The woman ordered a drink, one Finch had never heard of before. When it came, he saw it was pink and had a little plastic umbrella stuck in the glass. She sipped at it and said, "I've never seen you in here before."

"I haven't been in here in a long time."

"That so? Did you go straight or something and have now fallen off the wagon?"

Finch let out a laugh. "No, nothing like that," he said. "Haven't been in town for a bit. Just got back this morning."

"You mean to tell me you left this shit hole and came back of your own free will?"

"I didn't say that at all. Family stuff brought me back," Finch said, not wanting to get into the details.

"Family is good for that. Sucking you back into things you'd rather not be involved with."

"Don't I know it," Finch said. He spoke the words around an ice cube.

"So, you gotta name, or have you made it a point to remain handsome and mysterious?" she asked, removing the umbrella from the glass to trace her lips with the end of it.

"Finch."

"Like the bird?"

"Exactly like the bird."

"Darlene," she said, extending her hand toward Finch. They shook and Finch thought it funny that their meeting was so formal given that, in less than fifteen minutes, he'd have her in the back seat of his car, digging into her like somewhere buried inside was the answer to life.

"You look familiar. You sure you haven't been in here more recently?"

"I'm sure I look like most men that pass through here – desperate and a little bit pathetic."

Darlene laughed. "Don't forget self-deprecating."

"That too," Finch smirked.

"You wanna get out of here?" Darlene asked, sucking down the rest of her drink. She replaced the umbrella and set the glass on the bar.

Finch nodded, crushed one last ice cube between his back molars, and slid from the barstool. Darlene took him by the hand and together they weaved through the crowd, toward the exit, and then out into the parking lot where the crisp autumn air relieved the heat building in their flushed faces.

/ / /

Darlene and Finch sat in his car and made small talk, the rain coming on in bursts and squalls before fading off and then starting again. Darlene's hair was a wild mess of red tangles and slightly greasy with sweat from a long night of work. She let her hair fall into her face, hiding eyes that told more than she wanted them to. Finch just watched her, probably a moment too long, and she smiled, revealing teeth that were starting to yellow. She reached into her purse, pulled a cigarette loose from a pack, and stuck it between her lips.

"Do you mind?" she asked, motioning to the cigarette.

Finch forwent a vocal answer and instead dug into the center console of the car and came up with a lighter. He set the cigarette ablaze with a flame. The car instantly filled with a cloud of smoke. He cracked the window and watched a thin trail of iridescent fumes being sucked through the opening.

Darlene talked between drags of her cigarette, giving Finch the rundown on prices and what those prices included.

"Fifty will get you a hand job. A hundred to work your crank with my mouth. I usually charge two hundred for a fuck but, seeing as I think you're attractive, I'm willing to bring that down to a hundred and fifty."

"I didn't realize that women in your line of work gave deals." He sat in the driver's seat, turned slightly sideways to face Darlene. She flicked ash through the open window.

"Oh, for sure. I probably shouldn't tell the customers that, but you're easy to talk to and it sort of just slipped out. Don't go tellin' everyone," she laughed.

"Your secret is safe with me." Finch drew his index finger and thumb across his lips like he was zippering his mouth shut.

"Good." She ran her fingers through her hair. "Oh, also, for anal I usually charge based on penis size. But I hope that's not your thing because there's not a whole lot of room in here for that kind of activity."

"It's not what I'm looking for."

"Can I ask you a question?"

"Shoot."

She flicked her cigarette out the window and then rolled it up to close off any more rain from getting inside the car. "What's a guy like you doing with a working girl? I mean, you're attractive. Can't be too hard for you to get laid. I know why most of them need to pay for it," she said, pointing toward the bar to indicate the patrons within. "Mostly ugly with no personality, and the ones who are married are either tired of their wives and the same ole' position two nights a week, or their wives are sick of them and won't give it up but once a month."

"Sometimes it's not about paying for the sex, it's about paying to be alone afterward."

Darlene looked into Finch's eyes and understood the world of hurt that looked back. She had felt that same hurt and continued to feel it at various points in her life. A deafening silence hung in the air between them, and she was suddenly sorry she'd asked the question.

"So, what'll it be?" she asked, the silence becoming too uncomfortable, even for her.

Finch leaned forward and slid his wallet from the back pocket of his pants. He removed money and counted out two hundred in twenty-dollar bills and handed it to Darlene.

She counted it and said, "I told you a hundred and fifty."

Finch went back into his wallet, this time taking a fifty-dollar bill out, and held it out for Darlene to take.

"And what's that for?"

"You've earned it. Now just take it, and if you say anything else on the matter, I'll be forced to give you more."

She shrugged her shoulders and said, "Far be it from me to turn down more money." She accepted the creased bill from Finch and, along with the other two hundred, crumpled it all up and stuffed it in her purse before letting it slide to the floorboard at her feet.

"You're gonna get in the back seat now. Hike up your skirt and remove only your panties. I'm gonna strip completely and then crawl back after you."

She kicked the black flats off her feet and did as she was told, laying across the cool leather interior of the back seat. She worked off her fishnets, wiggling her hips as she did, and then slipped her panties off, letting them hang off one ankle. In the front seat, Finch stripped off his coat, followed by the rest of his clothes. Leaving his socks on, he slid over the seat, into the back, and onto Darlene. Their eyes met and she reached into her top to pull out a condom.

"In case you don't have one," she said.

Finch bit the corner of the condom wrapper, removed it, and sheathed his penis. He mounted Darlene, opening her legs, and slid between them and then into her. He worked his way through his own head, trying to stay in the moment. Sweat beaded on his forehead, his entire body following, becoming a furnace. He could feel Darlene's skin against his, a moist landscape. Finch closed his eyes and bit his lower lip, listening to the rhythmic breathing coming from Darlene. It sounded louder in his head than it probably was as he neared climax.

Eyes still closed, Finch leaned forward a bit, reached under the seat, and slipped loose the revolver, the weight of it in his hand feeling heavier than anything he'd ever held in that moment. Darlene froze upon seeing the gun and watched Finch place the muzzle to his temple. Her body tightened up. Then, in a fight or flight reaction, she began to squirm, smashing her fists against his bare chest, attempting to push him off her. Finch white-knuckled the revolver in one hand and with the other, placed his fingers on Darlene's throat, barely applying pressure, but she took it as a sign of how far he was willing to go.

"What the fuck?" Darlene lay frozen once again, her eyelids stitched to the top of her forehead. "I don't know what kind of weird shit you're into, but this was not part of the deal."

He shushed her and worked harder and faster toward orgasm. He jammed the muzzle harder into the side of his temple and felt the skin fold over the barrel's opening, felt his finger slide into the bend of the trigger. The next moment would be left to fate and if it worked out, his brother's voice, along with all the others, would be blown clean out of his skull. He readied himself and as he reached crescendo, he squeezed the trigger. The clicking of the hammer echoed out through the interior of the car, sounding just as loud as if the gun had actually fired.

4.

Tucker had parked the truck near the dock of the lake. He watched the rowboats that were hitched to the dock's pillars bobbing in the water, knocking against each other, the sound like two blocks of wood being banged against one another. The wind blew and raked the surface of the water. He sat slumped in the driver's seat, his head leaning against the window, feeling sick over the situation and damp with rainwater. He wondered how this situation even came to be. Closing his eyes, he imagined the road bending in a different direction – a thought that did nothing but make him feel worse.

He'd spent a lot of his life trying to understand where his father was coming from. Tucker had been left in a far worse position than his old man had to endure, with barely a pot to piss in nor a window to throw it out of, but still, the thought of suicide rarely crossed his mind. And when it did, he never dwelled on it. Unlike his father, Tucker's desperation, seemingly, did not have an origin in depression.

There is still time, Tucker thought.

Tiredness overcame him. He slumped further back into the seat, and he wondered how long he was going to have to carry the weight of three lives with no way of supporting them financially. Was anyone before him successful in rising out of the darkness when living a life like this? None he knew of. They were all either dead or in prison. How long could one man be his own light bearer? He used to think he could for as long as he had to, but at this moment, he wasn't so sure. He needed an out, once and for all.

Tucker pushed himself from the window and sat upright, the inside of his head cobwebbed with fragmented thoughts. One led to the next, causing him to zigzag through his own skull, his breathing fluctuating. It felt like something erroneous had stitched itself across his heart and exploded, dropping an awful weight into the pit of his stomach.

Peering through the windshield, he stared into the glare of a lonely lamppost that was cemented into the ground near a gravel walk path that edged the entire lake. A few yards from there was a sandbox with a play area made up of swings, a slide, and a few cast-iron animals set on springs for children to go wild on. In the summertime, this place was alive with locals picnicking and swimming with their families. His father had asked his mother to marry him here. Now it was a ghost and the body in the bed of his truck only served to prove that.

Just another lost soul to add to the pile of lost souls this town seemed to produce in droves.

The lamppost illuminated a dull glow that shone through the fog and rain, nearly hypnotizing him into a sort of calmness. The weight that had settled in his stomach began to feel a bit lighter, but there remained a free-floating sadness. His entire life, Tucker felt like he was mourning something, but he didn't know what. He was told that it was the feeling of nostalgia, but Tucker had nothing to feel nostalgic about. There were no better times to dwell on. His life had merely been surviving one day to the next.

He scanned the tree line that fringed the lake, looking out and imagining a world beyond it; a world he so badly wanted to be a part of. Unfortunately, where you're from determines what you are in the eyes of some, and that line of thinking was as good as gospel in Fulton. He was armed with a library card that he'd regularly used since he was eight and nearly twenty-five years of rough experience that no person should have to endure. Wasn't that enough? And how long was he going to have to pay for the mistakes of his parents? Like so many others, Tucker was no doubt the byproduct of a clumsy fuck, forced into existence only to be left to fend for themselves because people couldn't keep a lid on their urges, or at least play it safe. It was an absurd thought that never left his head.

BoDeen Carlson, wrapped in the blankets from the trunk of Rawlins' cruiser, had been placed in the bed of the truck like a deer carcass at hunting season. Tucker had known him damn near his whole life and now, even with the windows rolled up, he swore he could smell the cooked body of his only friend. The image of him melting into himself sprinted across Tucker's brain, along with the knowledge that one mistake is all it takes to make sleep an act of bravery.

Tucker cracked the window, put his mouth to the opening, and sucked fresh air into his lungs, the chill in the air feeling good in his chest. He relit a wood-tipped cigarillo that had been sitting in the ashtray for a few days and let the taste of stale vanilla coat his tongue and the inside of his cheeks. A quiet, forked lightning flashed across the sky in the distance and he chased it with his eyes. He wanted to hightail it out of there, foregoing whatever Rawlins had planned and return BoDeen to the scene of the explosion, or at least bury him properly. He had a family. Maybe not one that most people would see beyond the rural bumpkin trash they were, but he was their son and brother and they deserved to put him to rest the right way. Even those who've done wrong in their lives deserved that, at the very least.

Rain beaded the windshield. It came on in bursts before fading out again and continued to do that on loop. He leaned his head back against the cab window that looked out into the bed of the truck and said, "With you gone, how am I gonna keep cooking? I can't do it myself. There's too much product to haul. There were barely enough hands with just us two. Fuckin' Rawlins is already worried about this month's payout, and the supply went up with you. You stupid fuck. Why didn't you wait for me like I said? What the fuck happened in there?" He slammed his head against the window in frustration, a crack spider-webbing along the glass. "And now I need a new window. Thanks." Tucker laughed to himself. He was becoming delirious, talking to a dead body and laughing at his own jokes. Leaning forward, he eased his forehead onto the steering wheel and whispered, "Sorry, brother. For everything."

He took a pull on the cigarillo and thought, *Not a single person in this world has earned their birth, but some of us sure deserved our death.*

/ / /

Sheriff Lou Rawlins pulled into the parking lot of The Cat House, gravel crunching under the tires of the cruiser, and parked next to a Ford pickup truck, rust eating holes through its sides. It had stopped raining, but the parking lot held clusters of puddles and when Rawlins stepped from the cruiser, he planted his foot directly in one. His shoe filled up and his sock immediately absorbed the water. He cursed the owner under his breath for being too cheap to get the parking lot graded or paved. As he walked around to the front of the car, he spotted Darlene at the entrance smoking a cigarette, one hip thrust to the side in her usual 'I'm selling my ass' stance.

When she noticed him walking toward her, she shifted her posture to one that clearly said, 'I'm on the clock and don't need whatever shit you're about to dole out.' Rawlins had seen that stance many times before. After busting drug dealers and prostitutes as often as he did, you pick up on the body language.

Darlene threw her cigarette to the wet parking lot as Rawlins approached, slightly dragging his leg behind him. His knee was really starting to act up.

"You know what I've got?" Rawlins asked. He came to a stop and leaned against the wall to take some pressure off his knee.

"Shit for brains," Darlene said. "A two-inch prick?"

She waited for a response while a look of annoyance passed over the sheriff's face.

"I can play this game all night," she said and smiled.

"I have your boy in the front seat of my cruiser," Rawlins said. "Care to know why or where I found him?"

Darlene didn't need him to answer. That morning, she and Tucker had gotten into an argument about who was going to watch the baby. Darlene had gone off on a tirade about how she hadn't worked in nearly a week, and they were running low on funds. Tucker had argued that he and BoDeen had to finish cooking up their newest supply and get it ready for sale. In the end, Darlene won, but after Tucker dropped her off at The Cat House, he'd made the mistake of deciding to bring Toby along with him. It was something Darlene hadn't known at the time, but Rawlins being here told her all she needed to know.

"That son of a bitch. He told me he was going to stay home."

"Well, he didn't."

"Is he okay?"

"Who? The baby or Tuck?"

"Both."

"They're both okay, but I can't say the same for BoDeen."

"What happened?"

"I'll let your man tell you all about it. Right now, we need to get you and Toby home."

"Where is Tucker?" Darlene asked.

"I told you, I'll let him spill the beans. Get to walking," he said, grabbing Darlene by the arm, and pushing himself from the wall. He led her back to the cruiser where she looked through the window at her infant son who was sound asleep.

"You should really think about quitting this line of work and staying home to tend to your child. You're a mother, start acting like one." Rawlins walked around to the driver's side door continuing to lecture Darlene as he went. "God knows this kid already has enough working against him, doesn't need to grow up knowing his mother is sucking off his friends for beer money."

They stood facing one another, talking over the roof of the car.

"You're disgusting," she said, flinging open the passenger side door. As she got in, she scooped Toby up gently and laid him vertically on her lap, trying her best not to wake him. Rawlins slid in next to them, having to bend his knee manually to get into the driver's seat. He started the car and eased out of the parking space and then aimed the cruiser left out of the parking lot. The direction of Darlene and Tucker's trailer.

"Listen, I've had a fuck of a night, Lou. I really don't need you coming down there talking that trash at me. How dare you question my mothering. I'm doing what I need to do to feed my child. I love him."

"I don't doubt that Darlene, but you seem to think that doing what you need to do to survive and not being able to keep your legs closed are one and the same. You could just as easily wait tables."

"You know waiting tables don't pay shit around here. And what about you? After you take your cut from Tucker and Tucker splits the rest with BoDeen, we're left with next to nothing."

The thought of BoDeen's body flashed through Rawlins' mind, but he said nothing, keeping his word about letting Tucker tell her.

"I just need you to get off my case," Darlene continued. "I don't need it, not now, Lou."

"It's only a ten-minute drive. Can we get through it without the arguing?"

Darlene stared out the window watching the trees passing in a blur as Rawlins maintained a speed just above the allowed limit. "Yeah, sure," she said. "But for the record, you started it."

He glanced at her from the corner of his eyes and then returned his focus to the road in front of him. For the next several minutes, they rode in silence. Darlene held Toby tight against her knees as the cruiser rounded the curves of the road, bouncing in the ruts and potholes that littered the asphalt throughout Fulton County.

"What's got you so wound up anyway?" Rawlins asked, breaking the awkward silence.

"Are you asking me because you care or because you want more ammo to use against me later?"

"I'm asking you because I'm curious."

She sighed, reluctant to tell him, while also wanting to get it off her chest. With Rawlins, you never knew if it was a good idea to give him too much information about anything. A guy like him wasn't above using it to his benefit, but sometimes he'd surprise you with actual empathy that went a long way toward making someone feel better. It was always a gamble and never predictable.

"I had a john put a loaded gun to his own head while he worked at me from the inside," she said. "I'm still a bit on edge over the whole thing."

"What?" Rawlins gripped the steering wheel at the nine and three positions.

"You heard me."

"What kind of gun? What did he look like?"

"What does it matter?"

"It matters because if there's a lunatic out there with a gun willing to aim it at himself, there's no telling what else he's capable of. I can't have someone like that out there walking around looking for an excuse to pull the trigger. I need a description, so I know what and who to look out for."

"He was probably about six feet. Thin..." Darlene pointed her eyes upward while she thought. "...short, sort of messy brown hair. He had on one of those blue navy coats, the kind with the big buttons up the front."

"Any discernible marks, like scars? Facial hair?"

"No, nothing like that. He did look familiar though. Like I know I've seen him, but I also know I've never met him. You know?"

Rawlins slowed the cruiser, pulling off to the side of the road as he did so, and parked at the foot of the dirt road that led to the trailer. "You're gonna have to walk the rest of the way. With all the rain we've been getting, the cruiser is liable to get stuck up there."

"I figured," Darlene said, lifting Toby from her lap. She held him tightly against her chest and slid from the passenger seat. "Tell Mom I said hi and that I love her," she added, bending forward to look at Rawlins in the driver's seat.

"Why? She won't remember."

"Yeah," she said, her eyes showing a kind of sadness. "Do it anyway, please."

"You know you can come by anytime and tell her yourself, Darlene."

"Why? She won't remember."

Darlene closed the door and started to walk off but stopped and turned around. "Oh yeah," she said, speaking through the passenger window that was rolled halfway down. "The gun. It was a revolver. Slick looking piece, too. It had a kind of insignia branded on the handle – two arrows facing each other with a circle between the tips. It looked a lot like the Native American symbol for protection, like in the books Momma used to have around the house."

"Really?" he said, his eyebrow arching, a look of revelation spreading across his face.

/ / /

Rawlins called Pam on the radio and lied, saying there was no one at the scene of the fire when he arrived. He also told her to send Deputy Plank over to assist the fire department. It would buy him enough time to swing by his own place before heading over to the lake to track down Tucker and what was left of BoDeen and hopefully get some answers. If anyone asked why he wasn't meeting the fire department himself, he'd already have an alibi.

He pulled the cruiser up the driveway to his house and killed the engine. It had been a hell of a night already and the last thing he wanted to do was enter his home only to have to turn right back around and head out to fix a mess he'd had no hand in making. Or so he told himself. Lies work that way. Repeat them to yourself enough times and you'll start to believe them, forgetting they were never true in the first place.

There were two kinds of people in Fulton: working poor and dirt poor. Being the sheriff of Fulton County put Rawlins in a tax bracket that afforded him a house only slightly better than the rest of the population. His home was a three-bedroom brick structure built in the early eighties, one of the last to be built in what was now the only residential area. The rest of the county was peppered with trailers, condemned houses, and shotgun shacks, some of which had tarp roofs and people still living inside, pots and buckets littering the floors to catch any rain that found its way in, no doubt, and maybe used as an occasional toilet by the drunks that roamed the floors inside.

Land development had always been both a promise and a threat in Fulton. Large sweeping plots of land had been purchased and dug up, tilled, and turned upside down at the prospect that more money could be made. It gave people jobs for a while but then the economy tanked and all the suits in charge pulled all the financing out from under everything and everyone. It left the place looking like nothing more than a shadow of a ghost of half-developed land and unfinished structures and people, once again without jobs, were left to crawl on their hands and knees for handouts, eking out a life that was probably best left to die.

But before all that, Rawlins' father had been a deputy with aspirations of becoming sheriff. When Rawlins was in his twenties, his father answered a dispatch about a late-night robbery at a gas station. It had all gone sideways when Lou Rawlins Sr. took four in the chest. The suspects were later apprehended, and it was discovered that they'd only made out with sixty-five dollars and a case of beer. It taught Rawlins an important lesson, which was that life wasn't worth a dog fart.

His mother had been a schoolteacher who'd taught most of the population in town. Now she was a nearly blank slate, dementia picking away at her mind a handful of memories at a time. When she was diagnosed, Rawlins moved her out of her one-bedroom apartment at the low-income housing community for seniors and into his home so he could take care of her with help of a certified nurse, who he paid with the cut he took from Tucker.

Rawlins crossed the lawn and entered through the front door, thoughts about what Darlene had told him about the gun sliding through him like heated metal. Inside, his mom's nurse, Lucinda, sat on an ottoman reading. She wore loose-fitting powder blue pants and a shirt that matched. Her pin-straight black hair was pulled back into a ponytail. She twirled the end of it around her finger as she turned the pages of her book. Her skin tone told Rawlins she was most likely of Mexican or Puerto Rican descent, but she'd never brought that up and he didn't ask.

"Hey, Cinda," Rawlins said. He leaned against the frame of the door that led into the living room.

She looked up from her book. "Oh, hey, Lou," she said. "Didn't hear you come in."

"Mom do okay today?"

Lucinda nodded. "She did. Only a couple of fits, and she ate all her meals without a problem."

"Good to hear." He folded his arms across his chest. "I was wondering if you could stay a little late. I have to go back out, but I shouldn't be more than an hour or so."

"Of course. Is everything okay?"

"Yeah, just a few things I need to tie up before I call it a night."

"Well, there's no problem here. I'm happy to stay a bit longer."

"Thanks, you're the best."

Lucinda smiled up at Rawlins and he thought about how under those loose-fitting nurses' clothes was the body of a young woman he wouldn't mind having a go at. It had been a long time since he'd been with a woman. He felt an ache in his pants and quickly turned away to avoid a temptation that would ruin the relationship with the only other person who seemed to truly care about his mother. He headed to his bedroom where he changed from his uniform into his regular everyday wear: black slacks and a white t-shirt. He changed his socks, still damp from the puddle he'd stepped in, and put on the boots he usually wore while doing yard work.

Across the hall from his bedroom was his mother's room, the door slightly ajar. He peeked in and found her sound asleep. It was the only time she seemed to get any peace nowadays. Dementia is a cruel kind of death, taking from you what is rightfully yours and, really, the only thing most people have at the end of their lives while loaning it back in fragments, leading to a clarity that results in outbursts of rage and sadness at the realization of what is happening to you. Those moments were the hardest for Rawlins. Watching his mother regain memories and then trying her damnedest to hold onto them as they were ripped from her mind's arthritic grip.

He crossed the kitchen and through a door that took him into the attached two-car garage. It wasn't used to park vehicles anymore. Instead, its space was taken up with various gardening and carpentry tools, along with a lawnmower, stacks of months-old newspapers that

Rawlins was constantly reminding himself to get rid of, a workbench where he sometimes passed time playing Mr. Fix-It, and various boxes that contained his youth. At the far end of the garage, against a wall, was a metal shelving unit bracketed to the partition. He rummaged through the years of collected junk for a few moments before coming up with a roll of burlap that he used for blanketing the gardens out front and then continued his search.

If his mother wasn't alive, he wouldn't even bother with the gardens. It killed his knee and made his back ache to be down in the soil bent over for hours, digging and planting seed, but the flower beds that fringed the front of the house were one of the few things that brought his mother pleasure. On cool days, he'd sit beside her on the porch while she marveled at what was blooming and Rawlins would find joy in watching her.

At the opposite end of the same shelf, he grabbed a roll of duct tape and, along with the burlap, stuffed it into a knapsack normally used for camping equipment. He slung it over his shoulder and headed back through the kitchen, down the hall, and out the front door. He got into his personal car, deciding it was best to leave the cruiser behind, and eased out of the driveway, heading to where Tucker sat waiting.

First things first, he thought. *Get rid of BoDeen's body. Then I take care of Finch McAllister, that slippery fuckin' cocksucker.*

63

/ / /

The clouds had ripped apart and were etched across the sky like torn cotton swabs by the time that Tucker and Rawlins had moved BoDeen's body from the bed of the truck and down to the dock of the lake. Rawlins removed the blankets from the charred remains. The stars were out tonight, and Tucker stood with his back straight and head angled upward, trying to catch his breath from having schlepped the dead weight of his friend the twenty yards to where they now stood. His eyes traced the formation of stars that made up Orion. He'd once read that, at any given time, six thousand stars were visible to the average eye. Out here in the country, where there was very little light and little pollution, he thought it could have easily been ten times that many, and they always seemed to shine more brightly after heavy rain.

Manmade technology would never hold a candle to the brilliance of what Tucker held in his sight. He didn't believe in a God—not entirely—but he understood why, for centuries, humanity looked to the sky for their answers and their reason for being. How could you not? To stand under a vast expanse of unpolluted sky, one could easily come to understand how people long ago convinced themselves of a higher power, the beauty of the constellations bearing down on them. Only an idiot would deny its brilliance and sheer scope.

That was humanity's problem, Tucker thought. Science and technology distracting us from the bigger picture that was the absolute beauty of nature, and instead of embracing it, we destroyed it in favor of greed, cell phones, 24-hour news cycles, and more television programs than one could ever watch in a lifetime. He closed his eyes and sighed.

Rawlins stood hunched over, hands on his knees and taking in lungfuls of air. At his feet was the burlap and duct tape. He rubbed at his lower back, feeling an ache beginning to form, then regained his posture and said, "We need rocks. Ones heavy enough to weigh him down. I think there's some broken flagstone down at the foot of the dock that was used for fill when they built the damn thing." He waited and when Tucker didn't move, he said, "Well, go fetch some. I'm not dragging any more weight. My leg won't allow it, and neither will my back."

Tucker walked to the foot of the dock where it ramped down to a stony beach and sifted through the broken stones coming up with two decent-sized pieces of chipped flagstone. He hefted each one separately back to where Rawlins stood with BoDeen's body and placed them next to his friend. Rawlins moved BoDeen so he lay horizontal, heaved the stones onto his chest and groin, and then unfurled the burlap as if he were rolling out a carpet. Tucker slid the end of the burlap beneath BoDeen where Rawlins pulled at it from the other side until there was enough slack for it to be folded over to meet the stones. The two of them then began rolling the body up, stopping every few feet to make sure the fabric remained taut against the corpse, keeping the stones in place. Once the roll was nearly eaten up, they wound duct tape around the ankles and neck, and lifted the corpse, this time placing it into one of the boats.

After a few moments of stopping to catch their breath again, the two men were making waves as Tucker paddled them out to the middle of the lake. Tucker continued to stare upward at the stars while he worked the wooden slats, his shoulders and midsection beginning to burn, while Rawlins, ready to have a heart attack, tried not to fall over the edge of the vessel. He cupped water in his hand as they moved and wet his face to rinse it of the sweat dripping from his forehead and down his cheeks.

"That was my work out for the month," Rawlins said, the water cooling his face. He pulled a pack of cigarettes from his shirt pocket, lit one, and then tossed the pack and the lighter to the floor of the boat. He inhaled deeply, coughed a stream of smoke into the open air, and eased himself back against the inside of the boat, practically lying down next to BoDeen.

"I still don't understand why this is necessary," Tucker said. He had stopped paddling, having gone far enough. "Why couldn't we just leave him at the house?"

"It's better this way."

"For who?"

"For us. If we had left him there all sorts of cans would have been opened. We do it this way and it can be played off like he was never there to begin with. Like I said before, people already have their suspicions about the two of you." Rawlins slid his leg toward himself and draped his arm over his knee. He took a drag of his

PHILIP LOPRESTI

cigarette and then tossed the rest of it to the lake. "I need
to quit these fuckin' things," he said, coughing once
more.

"And what happens when people start wondering
where he is?"

"He skipped town. It's that simple."

"Nothing is that simple."

"That's because you won't let it be," Rawlins said,
pulling himself upright and maneuvering to sit on the
wood slat that served as a seat. He looked Tucker in the
eyes and asked, "Do you wanna be here to raise that child
and take care of Darlene? You think you're struggling
now, how do you think it'll be for those two with you
behind bars? I'm sorry your friend is gone if you can even
call him that, but this is what's best for us and our
situation. Like it or not, we're in it and it has its own set
of rules we need to play by, or we're both going away."

Tucker gazed up at the stars one last time. Part of him
wanted to put an end to it all right then and there, but
another part of him knew that Rawlins was right. The
fewer suspicions the better chance he had. Where there
was life, there was hope, he thought. As naïve as it
sounded sometimes, even to him, it was the thought he
returned to, hoping that one day it would prove itself to
be true. He'd learned to never vocalize that thought
though. It would wind Darlene up and she'd go off on a
tangent, something he hated about her, but also
something he'd never vocalized.

"Alright, let's finish this," Rawlins said, getting to his knees and bracing himself to lift the weight of BoDeen one last time.

Tucker joined him, kneeling in the same position and together they hoisted the body onto the lip of the boat before rolling him off into the lake. BoDeen hit the surface with a splash and Tucker watched him sink like a two-hundred-and-fifty-pound sack of failed dreams.

5.

After the incident with the prostitute, Finch was left with thoughts like, *Am I slipping like my brother? Is this how it began for Colm? How far will it go, and will I end up in prison too? And if I do, will I get Colm's hand-me-down jumpsuit?*

He drove around with these thoughts for a while, nursing a headache with aspirin and gas station coffee he'd stopped to get at Dagwood's, Fulton County's only all-night convenience store. When the landscape outside the car windows started to become a blur of ghosts, he decided to call it quits and drove over to the only residential area in Fulton, parking the Impala across the street from his brother's house. He sat there, laying his head against the seat, eyes closed until the headache had eased its way from his head.

On the front seat lay the gun.

He picked it up and toyed with it for a few moments, wondering how it would have all played out had the chamber been loaded. Would Maggie and Sarah cry for him the way they would probably cry for his brother? Would Colm catch wind of it before they put him down, and, if he did, how would he react? Would he go quiet, thinking someone was there to meet him on the other side? Or would his sadness take the form of anger, to which the guards would be on the receiving end?

All the lights were off except for the dull glow of a nightlight coming from a window off to the left on the second floor. It was Sarah's room. That much he remembered. Three years isn't a long time in the grand scheme of things, but it can feel like an eternity when you've spent most of it alone and inside your own head with nothing but your own bad thinking to keep you company.

Finch had bought the nightlight for Sarah the day Colm was sentenced to death. He told her it would keep any nightmares at bay, for which there were many. Finch understood that and it broke his heart having to watch a five-year-old girl struggle with ideas and feelings she was too young to comprehend. She didn't know the full extent of the situation, but she knew Colm would not be coming home. Ever. She asked if it was something she'd done. She asked if she was being punished for something and, if she apologized, could he come home. What is there to say to that? How do you explain to a five-year-old who is bawling her eyes out that nothing she ever did could compare to the actual reasons she would never see her father again, no matter how much she promised to be good?

Finch let the gun fall from his grip, his hand feeling a phantom weight long after he dropped it, knowing this came from the significance the gun possessed. Soon, Rawlins would learn of his return, and it would be Finch's ass on the line.

He returned the gun to the glove compartment and stepped out of the car, crossed the street, and traversed the lawn, a low-lying fog drifting just above the well-manicured grass as he moved. An owl from somewhere in the surrounding trees made itself known. Down the street, a faulty muffler cut through the still silence and stopped Finch in his tracks. He held his breath, waiting for the sound to fade, then continued toward the house and onto the porch, where Halloween decorations hung and pumpkins were set out.

Picking a lock with what you had in your wallet was a lost art. A lost art in which Finch remained well versed. He remembered being a kid and learning the trick from his father.

"All you need in this life is a library card to survive," he'd said. "It'll give you access to all the information that you need, and it'll get you into houses where you can take what is necessary to survive." They had stood at the back door of their house and practiced until Finch was able to slip the card through the crack and have the lock undone in ten seconds. It would be another two years until Finch put it into practice. He'd spent a couple of times a week at that door doing it over and over so that when the time came there wouldn't be any mishaps. Now Finch stood on the porch of his sister-in-law's house and would see if the art of jimmying a lock was anything like riding a bicycle.

It was.

Once inside, he removed his sneakers to cut down on any noise while he moved through the rooms. Finch had always been naturally light on his feet and without the extra weight of his shoes, he could move through the house like a shadow. Had he chosen to burglarize when people were awake, they still wouldn't have noticed. It was the reason his father trained him as a second-story man.

Not much had changed since the last time he was there, save for the state of disarray. It told Finch that Maggie was most likely working two jobs now to try to keep up with the payments on the house, which he knew she was falling behind on anyway. This in turn meant that Sarah was raising herself when she wasn't at school. Laundry littered various surfaces—some clean, some dirty. Dishes sat piled in the sink. The corners of the rooms were dusted with dirt and the walls needed a new coat of paint. There weren't enough hours in the day to cook, clean, work two jobs, and raise a child by herself. They had been living the best they could.

Finch slighted his breathing as he mounted the stairs and made his way up.

At the top of the staircase was Maggie's room; down the hall was Sarah's. When he hit the top, he rounded the banister and moved down the carpeted hallway, walking his fingers along the railing to the end where it hit the wall directly across from Sarah's bedroom door. He was always grateful for carpeting when he crept a house. It made for lighter footing. Less chance of being detected.

Sarah was asleep in her bed. Having kicked the blankets off herself, she laid on her side with her hands tucked between her drawn-up knees as if she was huddling herself for warmth. Finch watched her from the threshold, her chest rising and falling with her shallow breathing. He stood for a few moments before stepping into the room. He covered her back up with the blanket, and then moved backward, retracing his steps as if walking back through his own tracks in a snowstorm.

Out of Sarah's room and to the left was the bathroom. Finch pushed the door open and, feeling for the light switch on the wall, illuminated the room with a flick of his wrist. Like the rest of the house, the bathroom was in a state of disorder with damp towels strewn about the floor and crumpled up clothing draped over the towel racks and the back of the toilet. He stepped in front of the sink and, for a moment, caught himself in the mirror's reflection. He averted his eyes, not wanting to face himself. He could have easily called and asked to see them, but instead, he took the cowardly route and crept through the house while they slept, proving to himself that he always backed out when he was most needed and that looking through people's things only made sense when it was prefaced by an entry known only to him. Growing up in the bent life surely skewed all lines of thinking.

Inside the medicine cabinet were various women's products, but it was the pill bottles Finch was interested in. He sifted through them, coming up with an array of anti-depressants, anti-anxiety, and sleeping aids. Most were prescribed to Maggie, but a couple had Sarah's name on the labels. Only ten years old and already living a life of coping through chemicals, he thought. It wasn't what Finch wanted to see. In a few short years, Sarah would be a teenager, and gazing at the pill bottles, Finch saw into the future.

It was one of heartache, denial, and confusion as Sarah blossomed into a woman and her daddy issues took the wheel. Her relationship with Maggie would go south and she'd seek comfort in bad men, looking for approval that only she could give herself. Maybe drugs would play a part or alcohol, and when she finally learned the truth, if she ever learned it, it would likely make things even worse. And who knows then. Suicide? Overdose? The thoughts were enough to make Finch claw at his own insides. He was afraid and he was desperate for both Maggie and Sarah to survive what was coming although he had no faith in either himself or the world helping the situation.

Down the hall, Finch tucked himself through the crack in Maggie's bedroom door. It was the first time he'd seen her in three years, and she was dead to the world and, most of all, to him. She lay on her back, snoring lightly, due to a deviated septum from a hit she took in the face during a cheerleading accident while in high school. It wasn't how he wanted the meeting to go, but he didn't know how to do it any other way. He looked at the dresser and picked up a framed photograph of her and

Colm. It was taken on their wedding day. It should have been him standing next to her, but in Finch's experience, life rarely worked in one's favor. He put the photograph back and turned to face the bed, his eyes finally adjusting to the dark.

If it had been him, maybe Maggie wouldn't be sleeping alone right now. Maybe Sarah wouldn't be relying on medication to help keep the nightmares at bay. But if it had been him, he'd probably still be living the bent life, maybe even in jail himself. No matter how many times he ran it through in his head, it always ended up the same: one of them in prison, the two girls alone.

Maggie had originally been Finch's girlfriend. They'd dated for two years while in their twenties. Then, like they always had when it came to Finch's relationships, things went sideways. Even now he found it hard. When she broke it off it left a God-sized hole in Finch. A hole that still couldn't be filled. He'd always considered Maggie the one that got away. Somewhere through the course of their relationship, a spark ignited between Maggie and Colm, and less than six months after breaking Finch's heart, she and Colm were dating. It was a defining moment in his life, Finch thought because it ultimately destroyed his faith in relationships from that point on. He spent the rest of his twenties doing everything he could to get into women's pants in an attempt to distract himself from the heartache. And once in, he did all that he could to get out.

Colm and Maggie married a couple of years later. Sarah followed sometime after that, and Finch was left wondering if it was Colm she had wanted from the start. It was a question that would never be answered because it was something he could never ask for fear of hearing the answer and finding out that their time together was just a farce. Nothing more than a simple way for her to pass the time. The thought of hearing that was too much to bear, but so was the lingering question. It ate away at him most nights, long after she'd married his brother, and often wormed its way into his dreams where he would strangle Colm to death, only to realize it was his own throat he was going for.

There was a slip up though.

A few years into the marriage, Colm found himself in the hot seat when he nearly got pinched while creeping a house. The owner woke up and caught Colm casing the place. There was a scuffle and Colm outmuscled him, but while he was rolling around the floor with the homeowner, the guy's wife had called the cops. If he was caught, it would likely lead to a sentence of three years, five with assault, but Colm had a gun on him which would have automatically jumped the sentence up to twenty-five with a minimum of fifteen. It was the reason their father had always told them to never enter a house while armed. Finch wondered if that was the moment Colm had started to slip. As far as Finch knew, the guy wasn't one of them. He didn't live a life of criminal activity. Finch had even dug around for a few days, hitting all the local haunts, trying to get the rundown, but he came up empty. The man simply wasn't involved in the same world as Finch and Colm. So why was Colm there? What was he planning?

Whatever it was never came to fruition because Colm took off for a couple of weeks to lay low. He told no one of his whereabouts, not even Finch. Maggie, whose nature was to be nervous, had confided in Finch about her concerns. She told him about his brother's late-night excursions, ones he wouldn't admit to, which was unlike him given that Maggie knew what Colm and Finch did. She knew more of their family history than any outsider ever had. But the conversation put the two of them in the wrong place at the wrong time. They wound up making love on the couch that Finch had bought them as a wedding gift and while they went at each other, Finch secretly hoped that his brother would never return, wanting to live his brother's life.

When Colm did finally come back, he swore to both Maggie and Finch that he was done with the bent life. And he made good on that promise. At least, for a while, until the night it all came crashing down in a collapse of screams and muzzle flashes and shifting blood through a badly wired brain. When it ended, four dead bodies were scattered across a suburban lawn and a fifth, the youngest of the family, was left floating face down in the bathtub, water flowing over the lip of the basin and acting as a metaphor: his brother's violence, like water, could not be contained.

"I was wondering when you'd show up." Maggie's voice startled him and cut through his guts like a filleting blade. Her head was sunk into her pillow, pushing her hair forward and framing her face in a way that made it look as if she were submerged in water. He watched her blink sleep from her eyes, made possible by the light of the moon coming through a slit in the curtain. The rest of the room was pitch black.

"Should have known you would wake up. You were the only one I could never sneak up on," said Finch, leaning against the dresser, his arms folded across his chest.

"What time is it?" She asked, her voice sounding broken, having just woken up from a sound sleep.

"Late. Or early, depending on how you look at it."

"You never did sleep."

"Night is when I do my best work."

"Still up to your old tricks then?"

"No. I'm an electrician now. Honest work."

"I'm impressed."

"Don't be. You've seen what happens when a man quits cold turkey what's written in his blood."

Maggie sat up, propping herself against the headboard. Her breasts spilled from the sides of a white tank top, her brown hair a mess from rolling around on a pillow all night. She ran her hands over her face to rub loose the look of sleep that was still present and yawned. Finch thought about jumping her bones right then and there, but it would only serve to make him feel even more hollow when she finally asked him to leave, which she inevitably would if she even allowed it to happen in the first place.

"Are you gonna stay after…" she stopped herself. She couldn't say it. Still, after five years, she couldn't vocalize it because hearing those words in her own voice would confirm what Colm had done, what he was underneath. Finch didn't blame her. He couldn't even look at himself in the mirror anymore. All he saw was Colm.

"Are we going to tell her the truth?"

"You know we can't. Not now."

"Then when?"

"I don't know. I don't know if telling her will ever be a good idea."

"So, we let her go on thinking that the man who fathered her is a murderer?"

"It's what she knows and she's dealing with it."

"Yeah, I saw how she's dealing with it stockpiled in the medicine cabinet."

"That's not fair," Maggie said. "She's doing well. She's in therapy and those meds are only temporary."

"Sure, until she can't cope without them, and its right back to the beginning."

"Give us a break. Or at least give her a break. She's young. She has time to process everything in a healthy way and come out clean on the other side. I mean, for fuck's sake, Finch, her father is going to be executed in less than a week."

"No, her father is learning about her by creeping the house and going through the medicine cabinets."

"Whose fault is that?"

"Not mine. If I had it my way, both she and Colm would have known from the beginning."

"As if the situation isn't fucked up enough as it is. We'd just, what? Sit her down and explain to her that the man she grew up thinking was her father is actually her uncle and that the man who helped create her is her uncle's brother? Maybe you could have moved in. We could have all lived here like some picture-perfect family." Finch stepped toward Maggie, into a slice of light the moon cast through the curtain. Maggie could see the sadness that always seemed to control and consume him. Brooding, as if it benefitted him rather than it being a detriment. "You've always been like an artichoke, Finch," she said, brushing a single strand of hair from her face. "A rough exterior, designed to push people away with a heart at the center of it all that is to die for. You're loyal, even when people don't deserve that loyalty."

She had a thousand corny lines like that. It was one of the reasons he'd fallen in love with her in the first place.

"Then why did you choose him?" Finch asked, standing firm, nearly rooted to the bedroom carpet. He drew air into his lungs and held it.

"Because women choose who they love the most." She paused, half expecting Finch to pummel her with hateful words—something she knew he did when he was hurting. He'd learned it from his father. When he didn't, she continued. "And in turn, men choose who loves them the most."

Finch was inclined to agree with her, but he didn't say as much. Men were fragile and sought affection from women. It was nature's way of ensuring the survival of the human race. Men needed validation. Without it, they'd be stripped back to their most primal selves; a bunch of Neolithic knuckle-draggers. Had life continued down that path, the whole lot of us would have been extinct before we'd even begun.

"Where does that leave me then?" Finch asked, finally letting the air from his chest.

"Somewhere in between. And therein lies the tragedy of you. You're existing in the present but living in the past, refusing to accept what is because you think you need to play the part of martyr. Nothing is written in blood, Finch. Nothing is set in stone. We all make decisions because we want to, and sometimes we're forced to deal with the consequences of the decisions of others. It's the price we pay to not live a life of loneliness. Everyone on this planet has things they wish they could take back or do differently. Some carry it longer than others and some never figure out how to stop it from weighing them down. Point is, we all have ugly shit to live with. You don't have a copyright on that. And constantly looking at your life through the lens of a tragedy that you could have done little, if anything, from occurring does nothing. Sarah will get through it. She doesn't have to live with the same heaviness you do because of what's happening in her life now or where she came from, or the blood passed down." She leaned forward, away from the headboard. "It's all so dramatic and ridiculous."

There was a silence so loud Finch wanted to hurl himself from the window and die on the front lawn. And in that thought, he had proven Maggie right.

"You never answered my question," Maggie said. She pushed the blankets from herself and swung her feet over the edge of the bed. She sat there, her hands gripping the edges of the mattress, and stared at the floor.

"Which was?"

"Are you staying?"

Finch didn't answer. He turned toward the door and slipped back out through the crack and Maggie just watched him go.

6.

Most of the area was overgrown with buckberry and Japanese knotweed, save for a tiny sliver cut out years ago, leaving enough room for a trailer. The trailer he shared with Darlene. Tucker had always meant to cut more of the growth back, giving them a bit more space, maybe some semblance of a yard, but time had gotten away from him and now it was a job that would take too much time and energy. The mere thought of it overwhelmed him and he didn't need another thing putting him on edge. And so, Mother Nature continued to flourish and make her claim, crowding the frame of the trailer.

Tucker eased the Bronco up the gravel driveway, the engine nearly stalling halfway. He cursed the forty-year-old piece of shit back into submission and goaded the engine like a well-worn horse being led through a well-worn land, parking just short of the trailer steps. He killed the headlights but left the engine running. The lights were on inside, which meant Darlene was still awake. He wasn't ready to deal with her and the blowback he was sure to receive from earlier events. It was bad enough having Rawlins breathing down his neck.

On the passenger floorboard, in a milk crate, was the batch of meth that saved his life, measured out and stored in respective baggies, ready to be sold.

Between his legs was an open tallboy of Keystone wrapped in a brown paper bag, which he'd stopped to purchase at Dagwood's on his way back from the lake. He had rolled the top of the bag down past the lip of the can and drank from it as he drove home. He took the last few remaining sips and tossed the empty can next to the milk crate. He gripped the steering wheel until his knuckles were bone white. A low drawl of country music drifted from the radio. He began shaking the steering wheel with such force he thought it was going to come loose in his hands, anger and desperation consuming his mind and body like wildfire sweeping through a field of dead pampas grass. Tucker screamed out, wanting to disappear. But he was being taken to task, not only by the local sheriff, whose boot was on his neck but by Darlene and the raising of a child as well. A child he knew wasn't his own.

Pride is a tricky thing. It could motivate a man just as easily as it could compel him to lay down and die. It could also make you naïve. There is no way to tell which way it will swing until it's too late and you're already caught in the throes. He'd seen it in all forms from men in his life—his father, his uncles, and even friends of theirs. As a child, he'd witnessed men who'd come back from war with a refusal to believe that the country they fought for with such pride had used them up and tossed them away like trash. They were always waiting on a better life because they felt they'd earned it. And they had, but those promised opportunities never came and the disability checks dwindled while their nightmares grew in number and they drank themselves deeper into denial. He'd seen some just as easily use their pride to lift themselves up and take chances with an almost narcissistic attitude, as if narcissism were a virtue rather than a defect, and he'd seen them prosper because of it. And then there was his father, whose pride became a burden too heavy to hold.

His entire childhood, Tucker watched as his father, bone-weary and hunched in the shoulders, do nothing but play by the rules and lose.

He shifted in the seat at the feeling of his guts twisting into knots, his own pride like a weathervane caught in a windstorm. He would never admit it out loud to anyone, but it bothered him that, although he knew how to fix a carburetor, the belt inside a washing machine, could hunt, kill, and skin clean game, and could break down molecular structures and carefully mix measured chemicals resulting in methamphetamine, he still found it hard to get a job that would support himself and his family. A job that wouldn't land his ass in prison. People like Tucker had skills that were lost on most of the country, skills that were dying as technology evolved, yet he was seen as a low life. The dregs of society. The thought of a guy living in California pulling in more than 80k a year not knowing how to change the tire on his 2020 BMW was insane to him. As far as Tucker was concerned, it wasn't racism that was the biggest problem this country was facing, but classism and the only color that really mattered was green.

He let go of the steering wheel and removed the mesh trucker's cap from his head. He wiped the sweat from his brow with the slick of his palm and wiped it on his jeans. He killed the engine, the music dying with it, and slid out of the truck, the driver's side door sounding like it was about to fall off. He went to the passenger's side and took the milk crate of meth from the floorboard, turned, and headed for the trailer. Distant thunder rolled off the surrounding hills as he mounted the steps and disappeared inside.

The walls throughout the trailer were wood paneling without much insulation between them and the outer shell. It did little in keeping the moisture out, with winters being especially cold and tiresome. Tucker had to cut and dry out enough wood for the stove to last them the season. The living room was set with mismatched furniture mostly found on curbsides with signs that read FREE on them. The carpet was puke green and smelled vaguely of mildew. The baby wasn't crawling yet, but that was coming soon, and Tucker would be damned if he had to crawl around on that mess. Whatever his next move was, it had to be one that got the three of them out of this shithole. Down the hall, at the opposite end of the trailer, was the bedroom that, for the last three years, he shared with Darlene and for the last eight months, he shared with her and the baby. They had stuffed a secondhand crib into the corner, next to a dresser, and coupled with the bed, there wasn't much foot room left to maneuver around the tightly cluttered space.

Tucker put the milk crate in a corner, covered it with a couple of towels that hung over the back of a nearby chair, then walked down the hall, his arm extended, dragging his fingers along the walls as he moved. The walls of the trailer were bare, which was just another reminder that this place had never been a home. He bypassed the kitchen and the bathroom and headed for the bedroom, where a shower curtain hung from the frame, acting as a door.

Inside the bedroom, a curtain danced, a light breeze blowing in from the open window behind it. He walked to the foot of the crib and peered in, his hands tightening around its railing, much like how he gripped the steering wheel. A dull ache began moving across the backs of his eyelids.

He knew the baby wasn't his. Even though he'd only made it to the eighth grade, the math wasn't hard to figure out. Darlene had slept with half the county on account she was a prostitute. That, and the fact she loved to fuck. There was no telling who the father was, but Tucker knew it wasn't him. He had once heard that a baby looks most like its father when it's firstborn. It was nature's way of telling the man that it was in fact his and nobody else's so the man wouldn't haul off and kill the thing. But Tucker had no plans on killing a baby, his or not. Even though he knew the truth, he wanted to raise him as his own. He wanted something to love and, selfishly, he wanted someone to love him. God knew he didn't get it from Darlene. Not the way he felt he should. She was too busy wrestling her own demons to ever truly love anyone, least of all herself, with a father who wanted no part in her upbringing and a mother who now barely recognized her, the child she'd given birth to. But Tucker subscribed to the idea that he had enough love to save all three of them.

He stood over the crib and gazed at Tobias, a ten-month-old ball of pink flesh that peeked out from a tightly wound blanket. The blanket was the same one Tucker himself had been wrapped in as a baby, swaddled against his mother's bosom. It was one of three things that were left from his childhood. The second was a chip his father had received from AA, which he kept around his neck, hung from a ball chain, and the third, a memory seared into the deep end of his brain. He'd learned early that sleep was a luxury and that dreams came with a consequence.

Tucker's father was a wall of a man, forged from equal parts gravel and grace. He was a farmer and he worked like a mule to provide for Tucker and his mother. He'd purchased a crop of land, but business had not been kind then and his father had been unable to make the payments. The bank closed on the land and the house.

Waylon Fodee had been ten years sober, longer than Tucker had been alive at the time, when he entered the house reeking of bourbon. It was the first time Tucker had ever smelled alcohol. It was also the first time he'd seen his father cry. He stood in the doorway, tears streaming down his cheeks, and, without warning, fired off a round from a .32 caliber, taking off the top of his mother's skull. Tucker could remember smelling firecrackers and gun oil as his mother was thrown backward against the couch and then lay there lifeless. His father soon turned it on himself and said, "There were only two bullets, which makes you either the luckiest kid alive, or the most cursed. Do with those words what you will." He jammed the muzzle under his chin, pulled the trigger, and painted the ceiling red.

He'd spent the rest of his childhood bouncing around to different foster homes until he ended up back in Fulton County where he tried to join the military but was turned down due to mental instability from past trauma. From there, he tried to find work, but the locals were afraid to hire him. The stigma from his father's crime still lingered and many feared he would follow in his father's footsteps and go off crazy with a loaded pistol. He stayed with BoDeen and his family for a bit and began a life of criminal activity. It started with stealing the copper piping from abandoned houses, which were plentiful in Fulton. He eventually graduated to making meth, using the same abandoned houses he'd stolen the copper from. And all that led him to Darlene who, in the first few months of their relationship, showed him more love than he'd felt since the death of his mother. Now she seemed to be slipping from his reach just like everything else around him.

Through the open window, Tucker could smell the rain-soaked surroundings. It was a smell he'd always loved, but now, like every other smell, it was muted due to years of cooking drugs. Even if he stopped cooking now, his sense of smell would always contain the lingering scent of burnt chemicals.

He kissed the baby on the forehead and said, "I'm gonna make you a promise and I'm gonna keep it. I promise that you'll never have to live like your mother and me. I'm gonna get us out of this." He closed the open window and went to leave the bedroom, stopping only to glance once more at the baby and turn off the light. He then made his way down the hallway, heart full of regret and shame.

In the kitchen, Tucker found Darlene sitting at the table, feet crossed at the ankles and resting on a chair opposite her. She held a cigarette between her lips and was flipping through a magazine she'd pilfered from the local gas station. Her wet hair was wrapped in a towel. She wore sweatpants and a t-shirt that was two sizes too big.

"Might be time to get a new magazine. You've been reading that one for a week now," Tucker said, opening the fridge. He removed a carton of milk and drank straight from the container before leaning against the counter to face Darlene. He reached for a box of generic cereal, dug his hand in, and came up with a fistful of puffed rice coated in sugar. He emptied his hand into his mouth, took another swig of milk, and chewed the cereal.

"You know I hate when you do that," Darlene said. She stubbed the cigarette out in the ashtray that was placed in front of her on the kitchen table.

"I'm starving," he said. "Why dirty a dish when eating it like this works just the same." He repeated the process a couple more times, then returned the cereal and milk to their proper places. He dusted the sugar off his hands and took his position against the counter again, waiting for Darlene to say something about his taking Tobias out while he and BoDeen cooked up a batch of meth.

"I'm not gonna say it because you know how stupid it was, just don't do it again. I don't need my brother showing up while I'm working to give me lectures. It was your turn to watch him," she said.

Tucker wasn't going to take the bait. He had a thousand things to say about what Darlene had just said and she knew it. He wanted to tell her she should quit selling herself, especially now that they had a child, but then he'd just be a hypocrite. It wouldn't do him or her any good if he walked through that door. He knew how stupid it was and the potential of it being tragic was not lost on him, but he was too exhausted to argue. Instead, he removed his trucker's cap, tossed it on the table, and said, "BoDeen is dead." He ran his fingers through his hair, not meaning to say it but realizing it too late.

Darlene looked up at Tucker, her eyes nearly stitched to her forehead. "What the fuck? How?"

"Place went up like war was happening inside."

She shot him a glance that said it all: It could have been the baby. It could have been you.

"I told him to wait," Tucker continued. "He didn't listen. I don't know what the fuck he was thinking."

"Where were you when this happened?"

"Outside, checking on Tobias and bringing a finished batch to the truck."

"For fuck's sake, Tuck!" She leaped from her chair and threw her arms around him, having to stand on the tips of her toes to get her arms around his neck. The towel on her head had loosened in her movements and it fell to the floor. Her hair hung in wet tangles just below her chin.

Tucker was taken aback at first. The show of concern was genuine, but something he hadn't seen or felt in months, and he embraced it with open arms. He held her tightly and breathed in her shampoo, remembering why he'd fallen in love with her in the first place. She had the ability to care and to love and when she did, he felt it immensely. It was just damn near tragic that it took something that edged on catastrophe for Darlene to see beyond herself.

"I can't tell you more than that. At least for now."

"What do you mean?"

"Let's just say you won't be hearing about a body tomorrow, that's what I mean. The less you know the better. All that matters is that Tobias is alright."

"And you."

"We'll see."

"What does that mean? Don't say that." Darlene unwound her arms from Tucker's neck and stood with her hands on his chest. He looked down at her, her eyes like freshly cut grass after heavy rainfall.

"It means I'm not so sure of anything anymore."

"My brother is behind this, isn't he?" she asked. She turned and reached for her cigarettes on the table, removed one, and stuck it between her lips, but didn't light it.

"Well, that much I can say because he's always behind it. Fuckin' guy has me by the balls. Has us both. I need out. We need out, Darlene. We can't keep living like this. I can't keep living like this," Tucker said, his eyes edged with tears. He turned from Darlene to avoid eye contact, a part of him telling him that he wasn't a man when he cried in front of others. He knew that wasn't true, but it was something he'd heard so much in his life that he couldn't help but think it. "I wanna tell him I'm done. Not just with forkin' over the money but with the whole operation. I wanna be done with cookin', which may just be the case anyway now that BoDeen is gone. He was the one that had access to all the supplies."

"Why don't you then? We can find another way. We always have."

Tucker sighed. "Part of me feels a sort of guilt knowing what he uses the money for. It's not like he's holding this over my head and taking a cut just for personal gain."

"It's not up to you to finance my mother's private nurse," Darlene told him. "He can put her in a home just like everyone else who can't afford the luxury of in-home care. Not to mention, while he takes a cut so my mom can live with him in his comfortable house, we're left to eke out a meager living in this trailer with nothing to show for you taking the gamble in the first place. It's you who stands to lose more because, in the end, whether it's him that takes you down or someone else, he won't lose. He'll find some way out of it."

"I know, I just always go back to thinking 'what if it was my mother'."

"Don't do that to yourself." She removed the cigarette from her mouth and placed it in the ashtray.

"She's your mother too," Tucker said. "You should want what's best for her."

"I want what's best for Tobias and us. My mother lived her life and she's nearing the end. We need to start living ours."

The window above the sink was open and the smell of something dead wafted in.

"We gotta keep this window closed. That smell is something fierce and getting worse," he said, changing the subject to avoid more tears and more humility. He turned and leaned over the sink to slide the window shut. "I'm gonna have to go out there tomorrow and see if I can find what died and get rid of it. The entire trailer is starting to hold the smell, and if I can smell it, you know it's bad." He gripped the edge of the sink and stared into the drain. He was being taken to task alright, and he was failing just the same. He was beginning to understand better why his father had done what he'd done, but he didn't want to give in to that darkness the way his old man had.

Maybe I am my father's son, Tucker thought, the mere idea making him want to vomit into the sink.

7.

Finch knew there was a bit of shadow in everyone, some more than others. The way he saw it, Colm had made friends with his own, crawled deep into it, and died there. What had he meant when he said he was making angels? It was just like Colm to throw something cryptic out there days before his death. Finch would never know. But one thing he did know was that Colm was able to whittle five lives down to a single memory, and that memory was of himself and the bloody rampage he gave himself to. He would be forever tethered to five people he knew nothing about and when people thought of that family now, they would only think of how they left this earth. They wouldn't think about a hard-working father of three or a caring mother. Nor would they think of the children and how happy and well-adjusted they seemed. They would think of the violence that robbed them of their lives, their future, and in turn, the last thing they would think of was the monster that took it all. In the end, Colm found a way to make it all about himself.

Finch knew exactly how it would go down.

Colm would be compliant up until they tried to strap him down. Then he'd go mad dog and erupt into a tornado of shit storm crazy violence. Not because he was afraid to take the leap, but because Colm always had a flair for theatrics. If he was going to go, he was going to find a way to do it on his terms. It would take no less, but probably more, than three guards to subdue him and in those frenzied moments, he would hurt at least one of them. What happened next would be anyone's guess, but Finch could see Colm reaching out and getting hold of some poor sap whose job it was to strap a madman to a bed, catching his tongue between his teeth, and ripping it loose from his face in one fell swoop. He'd chew it for a moment, for dramatic effect, then spit it to the floor and lay down on the gurney as calm as he was when they led him down the block.

They put you under before they execute you as if they're getting ready for some routine operation. Once asleep, they deliver the final blow in the form of potassium chloride which floods your system and shuts down the electrical signaling that all hearts need to function. At the end of it all, you are simply and quietly dead. Colm did not want the sedative. He said as much in one of the few letters he'd written Finch.

"All this nonsense with being put to sleep is pure selfishness on their part, baby brother. It's a way for the State to make themselves feel better about what they're doing. They claim it's

more humane that way, but I can't see anything humane about forcing someone to live in a locked cage with nothing but the thought of their impending death to keep them company, because you only get more frantic as the day gets closer. I just can't subscribe to the idea that gasping for my last breath could be worse than the day leading up to it. Although I must admit that if it must be done, I hope I dream of momma one last time."

Finch sat slumped in a corner booth in Dolly's, the diner next to the motel, and poked at his eggs with a fork, his mind turning somersaults, thoughts anxious and kicking at the inside of his skull. He'd gotten very little sleep and his guts burned. A metallic taste lingered on his tongue. The air smelled of grease and onions and made the sick feeling in his stomach worse.

A waitress holding a coffee pot came to his table and asked, "Is the food not to your liking?"

"Guess I just wasn't as hungry as I thought," Finch said, looking up at a nametag pinned to her left breast that read: *Beth.*

"Would you like me to take this plate then?"

"Please." Finch pushed the plate to the edge of the table, then said, "But I will take some more coffee."

She smiled and poured coffee into his cup, making sure to leave enough room for sugar and cream, before grabbing the plate.

"Thanks, Beth," Finch said, drawing the coffee cup close to himself and stirring in the cream and sugar.

"Sure thing," she said with a bright smile. Then she was gone.

He leaned into the cup, letting the steam envelope his face and he thought of Maggie and what she'd said about him being tied to his brooding. He thought about how other people's minds were wide open spaces where progress was possible. Like so many though, it was hard for Finch to realize a world beyond his own fingertips. Maybe she was right. Maybe it wasn't good for Sarah to learn the truth. Maybe that would only further her issues. Maybe it was better to let her go on believing what she knew was the truth. After all, history isn't always necessarily what happened but what has been written down.

He sipped at his coffee and in those moments between sips, made a decision. He would track down the money as Colm had asked, but instead of handing it off to Maggie, he would open an account in Sarah's name and leave it all to her, along with a note from Colm saying sorry. If Maggie was right about Sarah having time to work through her issues, then the money obtained when she turned eighteen would do her wonders. She could use it to live a better life somewhere else. Then he'd leave Fulton for good and never look back.

/ / /

While Finch sat at Dolly's ruminating on all that had gone wrong, across the street a faded gravel grey Plymouth containing two men pulled into the two-pump filling station. The car came to a stop at one of the pumps and the two figures emerged, stretching and bending to work out the kinks in their muscles from an all-night drive.

The gas station was a single clapboard square with a roof extending from its front and out over the pumps to protect people from the elements while they filled their vehicles. Beyond the gas station itself was a church, its hundred-year-old frame perched atop of a rain-soaked hill.

The driver, whose name was Clem Hazely, said, "This place doesn't even take credit cards at the pump." He turned to look at his friend, a look of amusement painted across his face in response to the relic where they now stood. He was a thin man, but solid, and wore dark blue worker's pants that hugged his legs tight along with a white t-shirt and a knee-length trench coat, black. The sides of his head were shaved damn near to the scalp, while a thick crop of dirty-blonde hair remained on top, giving his head the appearance of an onion. His face held thick-rimmed glasses and a smooth mustache spread across his upper lip, while the rest of his face was peppered with a five o'clock shadow.

"Whatta you care," his friend replied. "You don't even have a credit card."

"It's not for lack of wanting one," Clem said. "Anyway, I was just making an observation about the sinkhole we're in." He walked around the front of the car, digging into his back pocket to retrieve cash.

"You don't have one because it would be stupid to give a hardened criminal a piece of plastic he would never pay on."

Clem held out two tens, motioning for his friend to take them, and said, "You've always been the yin to my yang."

"You only say that because I'm black."

"I say it because it's cute."

"It's fuckin' racist is what it is."

"I'm gonna go with cute, but we can argue about it later," Clem said. He shook his hand, still holding the money. "Now take this to the person inside so we can fill up and decide on our next move."

"Ah, yessa masta, right away, sir," his friend said, as if he were a slave on some plantation, before jokingly hobbling over to take the crumpled bills.

"Now *that* was racist."

His friend, whose name was Abraham Lockwood, turned and made for the door of the filling station, laughing at the exchange.

A few moments later, Abraham stuck his head out of the entrance and told Clem it was all set to go. Clem pumped the twenty into the tank before joining his friend inside, taking note of a piece of wood fixed to a wire hanger that hung from the door. The crudely painted red lettering scrawled across it announced holy meetings in the old church out back on Sundays.

Once inside the store, Clem was greeted with a voice withered with age that said, "You two ain't from around here. Are you stayin' a spell or just passing through?" The man spoke the words from behind a counter. There was a rack of cigarettes behind him and off in the corner was a one-unit refrigerator stocked with glass bottles of cola and cheap beer. A single magazine rack stood in the store's center and a shelf that lined the wall in the back was crammed with various chips and snack foods.

Clem looked at Abraham, giving him a look that said, *can you believe this guy,* and then he turned his attention back to the old man who stood hunched, leaning on the counter. He wore a grey flannel shirt pockmarked with cigarette burns. His face looked ancient, the deep lines in his face giving the effect that he'd been whittled from wood.

"Think we'll be staying. At least for the night. That place across the street," Clem threw his chin up, motioning through the storefront window at The Blue Sparrow Inn that sat front and center of their view, "is it any good?"

"Good as any other place, I suppose," the old man said. "Ain't never stayed there myself, but from the number of cars in and out it seems to do business. Of course, that could just be the location. Ain't nothing on this stretch of road 'cept the place you standin' and those two places across the road. The motel is run by a family of Redskins. Good people. Nothing like the Indians I saw in all those westerns as a kid. Movies lie all the time. The diner there makes a mean meatloaf and mashed taters dinner. If that's your kind of thing. You all ain't no vegetarians, are you?"

Abraham held back a laugh and said, "No, sir, we're definitely not."

"Good. If there's one thing I can't stand, its vegetarians. Damn weirdoes if you ask me. We were meant to eat animals. If we weren't, why they made of meat?"

Clem and Abraham laughed, both at the surreal situation and the joke itself.

"Name's Hoffstetter," the old man said. "Jacob Hoffstetter, though most just call me by my last name or Old Man Hoffstetter. Been the proprietor of this here establishment for damn near fifty years."

"I'm Clem and this is Abraham," Clem said, pointing to Abraham before walking to the refrigerator unit to grab a six-pack of Keystone.

"And just how old are you, Jacob?" Abraham asked.

"Seventy-eight come next spring. Figure I got a couple years left in me then it's lights out for this old goat," he said. He picked up a rag from the countertop, wiped oil residue from his fingers, and then threw it back to the spot he'd retrieved it from.

"Well, I hope I get to live as long as you," Clem said, placing the six-pack of beer on the counter.

"Shit, if you knew what being this old entails you wouldn't be saying that in the first place. A little advice," he leaned forward, over the counter and closer to Clem's face, "Don't ever get old, son. Live life like there's no tomorrow because once your back goes, you'll wish yourself dead when it prevents you from bedding down some old broad and put the humpin' to her. If you know what I mean." Hoffstetter winked.

"I didn't think men your age got those urges anymore," Abraham said from behind Clem's shoulder.

"The fuck, son. I'm old, I ain't dead. My mind still works and so do my eyes. Not that I can do anything about it if the urge does present itself. Pecker don't work so well anymore. All it's good for now is pissin' and even that is a chore."

"Good to know," Clem said.

Hoffstetter looked down at the six-pack and asked, "Will this be it?"

"Can I also get a pack of Blue Spirits, filtered?" He pointed to the cigarettes behind the old man. Hoffstetter adjusted his glasses, took a pack from the slot, and placed them on the counter next to the beer. He looked up at Abraham who stood with his hands in the pockets of his olive-green mechanic's pants that stopped short just above his ankles where they met a pair of well-worn brown work boots that adorned his feet. He wore a white t-shirt that stretched across his muscular chest, red suspenders strapped to his shoulders. His hair was buzzed to the scalp, his face smooth.

"You a boxer, son?"

"Excuse me?" Abraham asked, leaning his head forward. He opened his eyes wider as if his ability to hear better relied on how far his eyes were open.

"A boxer," Hoffstetter repeated. "You ever been in the ring?"

"Can't say I have, sir."

"You look like a boxer. You have the build. Kind of reminds me of one I saw in my youth in Greensborough. Mean son of a bitch with fists like canned hams. Left the other guy on the dirt floor chewing his own tongue. It was certainly a sight."

Truth was, Abraham wasn't a fighter by nature. Even a five-year stint in Oakwood Penitentiary in Ohio didn't do to him what it did to most. He'd kept to himself for the most part and was nice to people if they were nice to him. But when taken to task, he was something to be feared. Abraham was a two-hundred-pound Negro chiseled from lean muscle that, when provoked, became fueled by the rage his daddy whipped into him as a young boy. A rage he could conjure up at the drop of a hat. Add to that a head full of liquor and he was a terminal menace to anything within reach. It was enough to steer clear because once that anger took hold, you'd find yourself going up against a serious piece of work.

"Eighteen sixty-three," Hoffstetter said.

"This guy is a pussy cat," Clem said, referring to Abraham. He handed the old man cash for the items.

"Well, he sure does look the part. Might be some money in it for ya if you ever decide to give it a go."

"I'll give it some thought," Abraham said, locking his fingers behind his head and stretching.

"Can I ask about the sign on the door," Clem said, changing the subject.

"What about it?" Hoffstetter looked up from the register and pushed his glasses further up on the bridge of his nose.

"Is that for real?"

"Son, the Good Lord ain't no joke and neither is that sign. The church came with the property back when my father bought it and it's been used every Sunday for service since. We get a full house most Sundays too."

"Good to know," Clem smiled.

"You two interested?" He set his eyes back on the register and began counting change to himself. "Cause if you are, strangers are welcome anytime."

"We might be."

Old Man Hoffstetter gave Clem the change he was owed and pushed the items across the counter. "Well, you two boys have a nice day," he said. "It was nice talking to ya and if you're still around this weekend, stop by and get some of the Good Lord in ya."

"We will certainly give it some thought," Clem said. He tucked the six-pack under his armpit and tossed the pack of cigarettes to Abraham, who moved quickly to catch them mid-flight. They exited the filling station and walked to the car.

A few moments later the still October air was broken by the start of an engine and Jacob Hoffstetter watched the faded grey Plymouth ease out of the parking lot and coast across the road to The Blue Sparrow Inn.

8.

Clusters of clouds had rolled in again by morning and they hung suspended like giant grey brains across a vast and endless sky. It was threatening rain again but this time it would not deliver, it would only cast a gloom. It was the kind of gloom that made you feel like you were walking in a waking dream, everything seeming slightly off as your eyes fought to adjust to the contrast of leaves and sky.

Lou Rawlins pulled the cruiser into the parking lot of the Sheriff's office and parked in his designated spot. He slid from the driver's seat and felt a pull of pain at his knee. He lifted his leg and bent it at the kneecap, repeating the process a few times in the hope it would work out the kink that wanted to settle in. It never did, but he always tried. Across the street from the office was a barren field and beyond that, a wide scope of mountains peppered with a thick crop of trees. Their colors popped against the gunmetal grey sky. He'd always loved autumn for this reason. The way nature went about dying was as beautiful as anything else the world had to offer. And she did it without a fight. Calm and quiet, she left her mark.

One could only hope to look half as beautiful as that when they die, he thought, but didn't revel in the idea for too long. He had other problems on his hands that needed immediate attention.

Inside he was greeted by Pam Tibbins, the dispatcher and secretary. She poked her head up from behind the partition that told everyone coming in who was allowed beyond that point and who wasn't.

"Morning, Lou," she said, her voice too cheery this early for Rawlins' comfort.

"Morning," he said, hiding his annoyance.

She looked at him a moment and he stared back, knowing what she wanted from him. She wanted to know about the previous night, but he didn't want to get into it. He explained it away by telling her he'd had no luck in tracking down Tucker or BoDeen and left it at that. He knew he wouldn't be able to hold the suspicions of the locals or his co-workers at bay for much longer. What had happened the night before really put a dent in the operation and the politics of it all were going to make a mess of his life.

He walked to the coffee station where a fresh pot of coffee sat, and he filled a cup. He took a sip, taking a moment to let himself feel the warmth as it traveled down his throat and into his stomach. He closed his eyes and silently thanked the man who discovered the coffee bean and when he was done with his little ritual, he told Pam that he needed to get some paperwork done, after which he walked into his office and shut the door behind him.

About an hour later, Deputy Plank knocked on the office door and was told to come in. He briefed Rawlins on what he already knew, but Rawlins sat and listened as if it were all new information, riding the façade like a pro. The cause of the fire was a meth lab explosion, no one was found at the scene, nothing was left of the house but a pile of ash, blah, blah, blah. He thanked him and Deputy Plank left. After he was gone, Rawlins took a bottle of aspirin from his desk drawer and ate a handful, chewing them to powder and washing it down with his second cup of hot coffee.

He sat back in his chair, the wood creaking as it fought to hold his weight. He put his feet up on the desk and thought about how he was going to get his snub-nosed revolver back from Finch. It was his father's gun, but there was more to it than the piece belonging to his old man, who was now dead.

Three years prior, Rawlins had made headway in connecting Finch to a string of burglaries—something local law enforcement had been unable to do before then. Drug dealers and thieves alike were beginning to talk and accept deals for spilling the beans. The McAllister family had gone on far too long taking from others what they'd stolen fair and square. Finch was in a tight spot with the heat coming down and he wasn't about to do time, especially considering what Colm had done. Finch would be put in general population where other inmates would find out who he was. Being related to the man everyone referred to as 'The Child Killer' wasn't going to make the stint any easier. He wouldn't last a week. So, when Finch saw the opportunity, he took it.

Rawlins was involved in the shooting of an unarmed black kid while off duty. He was leaving Westmoore's Pharmacy where he'd gone to pick up medication for his mother. As he rounded the corner of the building, headed to where he'd parked his car, Rawlins collided with a young black kid who was hastily rounding the corner from the opposite direction. They slammed into each other, and Rawlins dropped the bag, pill bottles spilling onto the sidewalk. The well-spoken young man apologized and, as both bent over to retrieve what had come undone, a voice came through the dark from down the street, sealing both their fates. The voice was that of a woman screaming about just being attacked. When Rawlins heard the woman's cries, he locked eyes with the kid, who knew immediately what Rawlins was thinking. Rawlins took the look of worry as guilt and because he'd been hurrying so quickly from the direction of the screams, he did the math in his head. But it was the wrong equation. When the young kid began to remove his hands from his pockets to throw them up and declare he had nothing to do with it, Rawlins again misjudged intent. He went for the snub-nosed revolver he always carried while off duty, firing off a round and hitting the kid in the chest. It killed him instantly. Upon further inspection, Rawlins realized the kid was unarmed, and in a moment of panic, he scooped up the bottles of medication and fled the scene in his car, unaware that across the street a local scumbag, Edgerton Tiggs, had witnessed the whole thing from an arched stairwell, needle in his arm.

In the coming days, Rawlins learned through his own office's investigation that he had misjudged the situation by an ocean's length. The young man turned out to be Grady Blevins, a twenty-year-old African American kid and the oldest of five who worked as a clerk at Dagwood's. He was taking night classes that were held at the local library. He aimed to get a degree in psychology, believing that better mental health awareness was the key to bettering society as a whole. He was on his way to the library and running late after being stuck at work, a job that helped support his mother and younger siblings. Rawlins was gutted, but he couldn't afford the publicity or trial. He had a promotion just around the corner due to the McAllister case and with his mother's health waning and showing no signs of getting better, medical bills were mounting.

The boy's face was plastered across local newspapers and news channels spanning the entire state for weeks to come, and even though his story was told, people chalked it up to violence committed by local criminal activity. In the end, Grady Blevins was seen as just another poor African American kid who'd chosen the wrong side of life, despite working hard to prove the opposite. With the capture of the suspect the woman had been screaming about that night caught and hauled in, Rawlins stashed the gun and never spoke a word of it to anyone. Instead, he let the mistake eat up what little good was left of him inside. It was a move that dictated his life up to the present moment. Every decision he'd make from that point on was one based on that night.

Finch caught wind of what Edgerton had seen that night. He was running his mouth to all the local drug dealers hoping they'd trade the info for scag, but no one ever believed him. Edgerton was known to be a person who would say anything to get a hit. He just wasn't a reliable source, but that didn't stop him from trying. Finch took the story with a grain of salt but figured it was easy enough to back up. All he had to do was find out where Rawlins lived, slip in, and have a look around. And he did exactly that. He found the gun stashed in a cheap safe purchased at a local hardware store hidden safely under the floorboards of a room lined with books. It was easy enough to crack and it gave him evidence on Rawlins in just under an hour.

He left a note with his cell phone number.

It took a week for Rawlins to discover the gun was gone. When he did, he called the number Finch had left and was met with Finch's voice informing him that if he didn't end the investigation, he'd turn in the gun. Knowing that every time a bullet is fired through the barrel of a gun it becomes imprinted with grooves and microscopic imperfections and that those markings are as specific to a gun as fingerprints are to a person, Rawlins threw his hands up and did exactly that. Finch took off and hadn't been back since, but he was back now, and he was putting it to himself, trying to blast one through his own head while humping Rawlins' sister. If he was starting to slip, where it would end up going was anyone's guess, but Rawlins needed that gun before Finch went off and did something comparable to what his brother had. It would be the nail in the coffin for Rawlins.

It made sense that Finch was back in town. His brother's execution was scheduled to take place in the next couple of days. That thought had occurred to Rawlins that morning as he stuffed spoonfuls of Farina into his mother's mouth and wiped away the excess that dribbled down her chin. Her condition had reduced her to nothing more than an infant. Not only did Finch's actions put a mark on Rawlins' back but it was also taking him away from the present moments spent with his mother.

Finch would be staying at one of two places: his sister-in-law's or The Blue Sparrow Inn. That much Rawlins knew. The next step was finding out which one and then figuring out a way to get the gun back without causing a scene. He couldn't do it by the book. He'd have to be as slippery as Finch himself.

Rawlins removed his feet from his desk and leaned forward. He sipped at his coffee, which was beginning to get cold, and cursed himself under his breath. He cursed the night he'd misjudged the situation, resulting in the last three years of his life being reduced to a waiting game, one where Finch had the upper hand and Rawlins sat around waiting for the hammer to come down. He cursed Tucker and Darlene for not having their shit together. He cursed his coffee for having gone room temperature and he cursed Finch and the day he was ever born.

9.

Even in his dreams, she wasn't alive. Instead, her corpse was propped up at the dinner table and Tucker was forced to sit beside his mother while a thin wisp of smoke floated from the bullet hole in her head.

"She kind of looks like a birthday candle you just blew out, doesn't she, son." Tucker's father would say. He was seated across from the two of them, his mouth a grin of teeth as he chewed, looking like a puppet gnashing at imaginary food. He'd then say, "Did you make a wish?"

He wanted to leave. He wanted to run away and hide and cry and plead and coax his mother back from death. He wanted to ball his fingers into fists and beat at the earth until it split open. Then he wanted to crawl inside and find comfort somewhere beneath the soft soil, but he couldn't move and when he looked down at himself, he would realize he was tied to the chair. He was forced to sit and watch his father eat, all the while trying to ignore the body of his mother beside him.

It was the same dream every time.

Tucker Fodee pushed himself from sleep and was met with the ding of his cell phone. He reached for it and found the spot next to him was empty. Darlene must have gotten up with the baby, he thought. He continued to search blindly for his phone, his hand doing wide sweeps across the mattress while he kept his head buried under his pillow, his mind still cloudy and full of the familiar nightmare.

Another ding, followed by another and then several more and Tucker pulled his head from beneath the pillow, fueled by frustration. He was assaulted by the morning light coming in through the window. Squinting against the harshness, he frantically turned over blankets and pillows, the act taking more energy than he had, and when he found his phone, he laid on his back, eyes closed, and nearly drifted back to sleep.

Another succession of dings came through and Tucker held the phone to his face with one eye open. The screen said 7:03. He checked the messages. There were sixteen in total, and they were all from Wilma Jennings, BoDeen's girlfriend, asking if BoDeen was at Tucker's place. Asking about what had happened last night.

"Fuck," Tucker whispered. He propped himself up on two elbows and ran his hand down his face.

The whole night Tucker had tossed and turned, finding it hard to get to sleep. He couldn't stop thinking about BoDeen's family. He thought about what was going to happen when they hadn't heard from him. He thought about what he and Rawlins had done and how it was far beyond making and distributing drugs or stealing copper wiring from the skeletons of houses. He thought about how this was going to come back to bite him in the ass, but he didn't think it would be so soon and he didn't think it would be in the form of BoDeen's girlfriend. This was only the beginning. Wilma Jennings was a persistent woman with a mouth to match and she wouldn't let it go. She'd ask questions and she'd refuse to take the answers provided because she'd know they were all bullshit. BoDeen always went home to her. She was going to be a serious thorn in the side of this cluster fuck.

Suffice to say, Tucker never cared for Wilma, but he had certainly tried and mostly tolerated her on account of her being his best friend's girl. But even with a low-level hatred for her, there was a part of him that felt a sense of sadness, and probably more than she deserved. She certainly knew loss. Wilma, like Tucker, had lost a lot.

Before BoDeen, Wilma had been married to a man named Stephen Jennings, a local loser who already had a few charges to his name by the time they tied the knot. But it wasn't until their son was born that he, like so many other people in Fulton, turned to cooking crank, and due to the endless supply always being within reach, it didn't take long before Wilma was sucking on the glass dick. It only took a couple of weeks for her to become a full-blown addict, which only got worse when tragedy struck.

Stephen Jennings was new to the game of cooking crank and, out of either sheer stupidity or just a lack of thinking, was keeping the potent chemicals in the refrigerator of their trailer. These chemicals permeated toxins that infected the food. Wilma didn't know that the piece of cheese she fed her two-year-old son was poison. She was too stoned to notice. A few hours later he'd become deathly ill and even then, it took Wilma another two hours to figure out how to get him to the hospital five miles away. By the time she got him to an emergency room, her boy was pronounced dead from a lethal dose of ammonia hydroxide. Wilma rolled on Stephen and all the buyers she knew of and in exchange, she avoided prison time for neglect that led to the demise of a child. After that, she crawled further into her addiction which landed her BoDeen's lap, as if her addiction had a sentient gift of sniffing out the person who would not only allow it to continue but feed it in the process.

Tucker stared at his phone. The last message she'd sent read: I'M COMING OVER.

He crawled out of bed and took a longer shower than he normally would have, standing under the nozzle and letting the hot water rush him in an attempt to wash away the feeling of the previous night's events. Afterward, he changed into a fresh pair of jeans and a black t-shirt. He stood in front of the bathroom sink, toothbrush hanging from his mouth, and stared at the steam-covered mirror. Somewhere behind the condensation was his reflection, but he didn't bother wiping it away. Instead, he envisioned what he wanted to see. A man who didn't live hand to mouth. Who slept through the night and woke in the morning with a clear conscience and little regret. He imagined a man who felt he had a purpose, but most of all a man who loved and felt loved. He spit into the sink, replaced his toothbrush in the coffee cup that also held Darlene's toothbrush, and drew a smiley face in the steam smeared mirror where his face should have been.

Darlene was sitting on the living room couch when Tucker entered from the hallway. She had Tobias in a highchair and was feeding him baby food from a jar. It was clear from the look on the child's face that he was not enjoying it.

"He likes crushed pears," Tucker offered.

"I know, Tuck, but he can't just live on pears."

"Why not? You live on coffee and cigarettes," he teased, smiling, as he picked up his mesh trucker's cap from the armrest of a chair. He slapped it against his knee to dust it off and then adjusted it on his head.

Darlene rolled her eyes and shook her head slightly, deciding it wasn't worth it to come up with a response. She watched Tucker walk to a hook that was driven into the wall near the door. He took his olive-green army jacket from it and wiped off the sleeve, trying to remove some of the soot before slipping himself into it.

"Wilma's on her way."

"What? Now? Why?" Darlene shot off the words in rapid succession before turning her attention back to

Tobias. She wiped his chin clean of excess baby food with the spoon.

"She's been blowing up my damn phone asking about BoDeen."

"What did you tell her?"

"Nothing yet."

"Why not?"

"What the fuck am I gonna tell her? And don't say 'the truth' because that is not an option," Tucker said. "I already took a gamble telling you what little I did."

"What is that supposed to mean?"

"That I probably shouldn't have said shit because I don't want you involved in this."

"Too late for that."

"Just don't say anything to your brother or Wilma. Please."

Darlene crossed her heart with her pinky finger and then kissed the tip and held it out for Tucker to complete the ritual.

"Really? A man is dead, and you're going to reduce it to a child's game of pinky swear?"

"Pinky swearing ain't no game, Mr. Fodee. It is a serious gesture of trust. If I break this promise, I could die," she said, smiling, trying to lighten up the situation even though inside she was just as wound as Tucker.

"A smart ass even when the situation is at its bleakest."

"That's me." She turned back to feeding Tobias, waited a five count, and then added, "Could have at least told her not to come by this early."

"You know that wouldn't have done any good. Wilma is gonna do what Wilma is gonna do. Woman is nuttier than squirrel shit with a mouth that runs like a chicken's ass to boot. But you know this and it's probably the reason you said what you said."

"And the cycle begins again."

The sound of tires rolling across frosted mud and fallen leaves caught their attention.

Tucker looked out the window to see Wilma Jennings' blue Toyota coming up the drive. She parked it next to the Bronco and was leaping from the driver's seat and running up the trailer steps in seconds. Tucker opened the door before she had a chance to knock. She looked ragged, like a woman who hadn't slept in days. No doubt she'd been up all night, her mind racing while she smoked the rest of BoDeen's supply. Her fading black hair was pulled into a greasy ponytail, her face cut with deep lines from age. She wore sweatpants two sizes too big and one of BoDeen's old hoodies, the sleeves starting to become rags. Sores blotted the rim of her lips.

She got inches from Tucker's face, looked him directly in the eyes, and said, "Where the fuck is he?"

"I don't know, Wilma," Tucker said, leaning back to stave off the smell of rotting teeth that lined her mouth at odd angles.

"Bullshit," she said, just as Tucker had predicted, but he had no choice other than to continue with his plan at this point, which was to just play dumb. Handling it any other way would only lead to one outcome and that just wasn't an option.

"Lower your voice," Tucker said, running his tongue along his teeth trying to imagine what it was like to have that much rot only a few inches from his brain.

"Lower my voice?" She lifted her chin to the sky and said, "You hear this? He wants me to lower my voice," as if she were talking to God, her voice becoming more frantic and louder than when Tucker told her to keep it quiet. "My man doesn't come home and then I catch wind of a house fire," she said, stepping into the trailer and putting her finger in Tucker's chest, "where you two were supposed to be, and now I'm supposed to just stand here and whisper and remain calm?"

Tucker could feel her finger pressing into his father's AA chip, which hung around his neck. He shooed away her hand and said, "I have a baby in here, so if you wanna talk that's fine, but if you're gonna raise your voice and scream, well you can just turn around, get back in your car and drive on outta here. You will not, under any circumstance, upset this child."

It was a side of Tucker that Wilma had never seen before.

Neither had Darlene.

She looked up from the couch at the two of them standing near the doorway. He was being assertive and dominating, the tone in his voice coming from some previously untapped place that Darlene hadn't realized existed. Tucker had always been complacent, happy to go along with others. It wasn't because he was afraid of what they might do or say, but because he was afraid of what he might do. He held a deep rage in him, and it took all he had to keep it at bay. If he let go, there was no telling how far it would take him.

Darlene liked this side of him. She sat up straighter and locked eyes with Wilma for a few moments.

"Where the fuck is he, Tuck?" This time she whispered the words and Tucker saw her eyes go wet.

"I don't know. He fucked up. He fucked it all up. I told him not to touch anything, next thing I know the place is about to blow and we got out of there. He took off. I got in my truck, and I came home. That's all I know."

"This just doesn't seem right. It's not like him," Wilma said. "Hell, it's not like *you* to just leave him behind."

"Maybe not, but it's what happened," Tucker insisted. He looked past Wilma at the Bronco that was visible through the open door. He couldn't look her in the eyes, and that was something she picked up on right away. A look of distrust and revelation flashed across her face.

"You son of a bitch," she hissed. "You fuckin' no good rotten son of a bitch. I'm gonna get to the bottom of this and when I do, you and that harlot of yours are gonna be the first to fall." She turned and walked back through the open door and down the trailer steps.

Tucker followed, stopping at the threshold. "You do what you have to do," he said, "but don't come back here looking to start trouble. I don't wanna hear nothin'. And later, when you're jonesing for a hit because you smoked up all of BoDeen's stash, remember I told you to go fuck yourself." He slammed the door shut. A few moments later the sound of her car filled the trailer before drifting off as she disappeared down the driveway.

Tucker turned, yelled, "Fuck!" and swatted an empty can of Dr. Pepper off a table on his way to retrieve his phone from the bedroom.

10.

They made love in the shower. Far from the other inmates. Far from prying eyes that would sneak glances while they handled themselves to climax and guards who would break it up were they caught in a coital embrace in the laundry room. And when they were finished, Clem Hazely stood in the doorway of the bathroom toweling off. He thought about how free he felt, not only because he was no longer behind bars and didn't have to answer to any of the fuck-face guards who hated their jobs and their wives and themselves and who, in turn, made his own life more of a living hell, but also because he could fuck the man he loved whenever he wanted. He could fall asleep beside him without remarks of bigotry or others trying to get in on the action. And when he was done soaking in that thought and done drying off, he redressed in the same clothes he'd worn earlier: dark blue mechanics pants and a white t-shirt. He sat in a chair in the corner of the room and cracked open a beer, smiling at his freedom.

Abraham sat on the bed, his skin still slick with condensation, a towel wrapped around his waist. He sipped from a can of Keystone and loaded rounds into a sawed-off shotgun, his muscles flexing every time a shell entered the chamber. Clem took in the sight with great vigor. *A beautiful African Goddess*, he thought. His groin ached. He wanted to have another go, this time on the floor, but he did his best to clear his head. Other things needed to get done.

"Are you sure about this one, Clem?"

"Why wouldn't I be?"

"He just seems a bit old."

"Ain't that sweet of ya. But age is not a factor in this mission. It happens tonight, no exceptions. It's the perfect place. Secluded, quiet, and the only station between two towns, so you know the till is full up with the foot traffic they get all day," Clem said, taking a swig from the can of beer. "And did you hear him about the church out back?"

"I heard him, Clem."

"Might be a bit of extra cash in this one, donation box and all," he pointed out. Clem stood from the chair, walked to the door, and opened it. He looked out at the motel parking lot and across the street at the two-pump station. He lit a cigarette and blew streams of smoke from the side of his mouth. "Old man was a character though, wasn't he?"

"Sure was," Abraham said.

Clem looked over his shoulder at Abraham and noticed a look of concern on his face. He tossed his cigarette to the parking lot, shut the door, and moved to the bed, sitting down next to Abraham.

"Hey," Clem said, putting his hand on Abraham's knee. Abraham lifted his eyes from the task at hand and looked at Clem. "I'm doing this for you. For us."

"I know and I appreciate that, but he's old," Abraham said, his gaze moving to the floor. "Don't feel right about taking from an old man. My father is about that age."

"Your old man whipped the tar out of you your entire life," Clem said, a forceful jolt of anger buried behind the words. "And then when he found out who you were" — 'wasn't what he wanted you to be, he beat you harder. Then to add insult to injury he ratted you out which directly led to your incarceration. Don't let this opportunity stir up old ghosts you have about your old man. I hate seeing you hold onto that baggage. You have enough going on up there," Clem tapped Abraham's head, "You don't need to be schlepping around the weight of a man that don't give a damn about you."

"You don't need to remind me."

"Apparently, I do."

Abraham rested the shotgun on the bed between him and Clem. "It's just not how I wanted this to go. I did my time and told myself I was done."

"Time you didn't even deserve, not as much time as you served anyway, and the only reason you did serve that much time is because you're black."

"Let's not get into that discussion."

"Why? Doesn't it bother you?"

"Of course it does, but sitting around being pissed off at the world isn't going to change what happened and I don't need *you* being mad *for* me because, while I appreciate you going to bat in my defense, white people overly advocating for blacks only makes the situation worse. Good deeds will not end systemic racism. You know my stance on this." Abraham shrugged his shoulders. "Besides, you know better than anyone that behind prison walls it doesn't matter the color of your skin. We're all niggers in the eyes of the rest of the world."

"Well if being a *nigger* means I continue on with the plan until we have enough so the operation can be paid for and your needs are met, then I don't want to be white." Clem said.

They stared at each other in silence for a few moments, knowing that both wanted the same thing but with different approaches.

"Listen," Clem took Abraham by the chin and looked into his eyes, "I wanna be done too. I'm ready to settle down and live quietly. You changed that in me. Before you, I was a time bomb and I detonated at any given moment, but you know ain't no one gonna give two cons a job that would allow us to pay bills and save up for that kind of operation. This is the only way and until then, I'm still a criminal."

For the past three months, Clem and Abraham had been riding across the country keeping a low profile by knocking over two-bit gas stations. The idea came to

Clem while the two lay in bed, having just made love. It was when all his ideas came to him. It had only been a couple of months since their release from prison and he was trying to devise a way to come up with the money they needed and avoid going back to the slammer in the process. He figured if they kept to back roads and knocked off small filling stations, they'd have a better chance of not being caught. With banks being too risky, they decided to hit the kind of places that didn't have good security and that were operated by one or two people at a time. It would take longer to raise the money, but it could pay off. And it was paying off. In just three months they had swept through five states. They held up a few at a time, then they would lay low for a handful of days before repeating the process. And they would continue to repeat the process until their goal was reached. Clem would see to it.

But Abraham had been resistant from the beginning. He knew that Clem was right about not being able to land jobs that would pay them enough. He just wanted to be done with it all. He wanted the operation so he could start his life as a woman, finally looking on the outside the way he'd felt on the inside since he was a young man. Clem was the first person with whom he'd ever divulged at length his affliction. As hardened as he was, Clem accepted people for who they were with very few questions, if any at all. It was one of the reasons Abraham had fallen in love with him and although what they were doing was seen as criminal, Clem was doing it out of pure selflessness. He was risking going back to prison so

Abraham could fulfill his need and finally be who he truly felt he was. Call him what you wanted, but to Abraham, that was true love and no one could convince him otherwise.

But still, Abraham was worried. There was no telling what a man would do when they had a hand grenade for a heart. Clem stood at only 5'7", and although he was lean and fit, he wasn't naturally muscular the way Abraham was. It took more than muscle for people in prison not to fuck with you and in Clem's case, he had it. He was a wild card of a convict. The kind that other hardened criminals avoided when possible. He held no code and could snap at any moment for seemingly no reason, and when you least expected it. Other times, he'd offer a friendly hand when you thought he'd be throwing fists. When the world has been nothing but cruel and ugly to a man, a man would give it back any way he could.

Clem leaned in and pressed his forehead against Abraham's and said, "We're almost there. Just a little bit longer."

/ / /

The curtains were drawn against the harsh sunlight coming through the thinning trees. Clem and Abraham spent the day sitting around in the dim motel room smoking and drinking beer, cleaning and loading the guns, and biding their time with bad television, cold cans of stew, and catnaps, waiting until it was time to put their plan into action which involved Clem taking the risk and Abraham staying behind in case something went wrong. This was pretty much how it had been since the beginning of the spree. Clem didn't want Abraham getting caught up in some mess if things went south so he usually waited in the car or a motel room while Clem pulled off the actual job. If things did go wrong, Abraham would be able to get away with the money they had already accumulated and from there, find a way to come up with the rest. Abraham had told Clem he wouldn't be able to do it without him, but Clem assured him that it was the best way. If they were both in prison, then Abraham's dream of becoming a woman would never come to fruition.

The old man had said the store closed at nine so Clem would head over a few minutes before, slip in, and act sorry for popping in so close to closing time. Once the exchange between himself and Hoffstetter played out, Clem would make his move. Then they'd load their haul into the Plymouth and drive through the night until they felt they'd put enough miles between them and the crime scene.

"What about Bernadette?" Clem asked. He was lying on his back, staring at the ceiling.

Abraham rolled over, propped himself up on one elbow, and looked into Clem's eyes. They were a rheumy sort of blue, like the gravel sunk to the bottom of an aquarium, and they were one of the only things that got him through his five-year prison sentence for being the lookout on a botched robbery. They made him think of the ocean, a place he'd only ever seen in pictures, but one that he wanted to visit. And until then, Clem's eyes would do.

"You can't be serious."

"Just a suggestion."

"An ugly one."

"Yeah, I guess it kind of is. I knew a woman with that name when I was a kid. She lived next door to me and my family and she would stand on her porch and yell shit in Polish. No one knew what the hell she was saying or who she was directing it at, but she was a fat slob of a thing," said Clem. "She always had sweat stains in her armpits. Even in the winter. I think her husband offed himself."

"Lovely. So, what you're saying is that every time you fuck me, you wanna think of fat Polish women?" Abraham asked.

"Now you got me thinking I may have a fetish I didn't know existed," Clem said, reaching for the cigarettes on the bedside table. He lit one and placed an ashtray on his stomach.

Abraham looked down at Clem's shirtless torso, his chest permanently marred by a prison tattoo and one that wasn't particularly well done. It was just thin, crudely inked lines spelling out the words: I BLAME SOCIETY.

"Maybe when I get my op, we can spend a little more on getting rid of this ugly ass tat," Abraham said, grazing the lettering along Clem's skin with his fingertips. The lines felt raised, almost like Braille.

Clem stuck the cigarette in the corner of his mouth, letting it dangle as he talked. "Hey, Vladislav the Russian gave me this," he pressed at the letters with his fingertips. "Used a safety pin taped to the end of a popsicle stick and ink that was stolen from the prison library. It was free too. I was his guinea pig."

"No shit, it shows."

"I like it." Clem sucked back a drag on the cigarette but didn't remove it from between his lips, just blew the smoke from the other side of his mouth. He squinted through the trails of smoke that crawled up his face and said, "I like the statement. All the talk of people being crazy and the mentally ill, maybe it's our environment that's sick."

Abraham plucked the cigarette from Clem's mouth and took a drag, then placed it in the ashtray. He didn't want to get into a social and philosophical discussion right now. They never ended well, especially when Clem was on the other end of them, so he went along with it the only way he knew how. "I suppose if I can get my dick cut off and not hear a thing from you about it then you can keep the ugly tattoo."

"Fair deal," Clem said and threw a wide smile.

11.

She'd been referred to as "The Miracle Child" nearly her whole life, not only by her mother but also by aunts, cousins, and teachers. Even her mother's friends who came by the house on Sunday afternoons to talk about the books they were reading while they sat at the kitchen table drinking tea. The only person that hadn't called her that at any point in her life was her brother, Louis.

Lynette Rawlins had gotten pregnant a second time when she was damn near in her sixties, long after she thought it was possible, nature having taken its toll. Rawlins was in his twenties and his father dead three years when she'd become smitten with a new man by the name of Wydell Buford. He was a man who, on the outside, didn't appear particularly interesting but somehow, he held the attention of Lynette. It didn't last though. Not long after learning that her belly would soon be swollen with a child, he took off, never to be heard from again. The only thing Lynette ever said on the matter was, "Lou, they can't all be as great a man as your daddy," and she put her hand on his and kept it there while they sat gazing at the sunset together from the porch of the house where Rawlins had lived his entire childhood.

And now, all these years later, he'd once again proven his mother right. But this time it wasn't just a stranger that couldn't fill his father's shoes, but his own blood. Rawlins himself. He was hooked up in a bad situation and couldn't for the life of him figure out how it came to be. He tried mapping the events, but it all became a twisted mess with no discernable difference between where one event ended and the other began, one bad decision bleeding into the next like ink spreading and blooming through tissue paper.

After driving by The Blue Sparrow Inn and spotting the Impala, a car he remembered well, he turned around in the parking lot of the two-pump filling station and drove over to Tucker and Darlene's. He eased the cruiser up the swath of dirt and gravel, the rough terrain jostling him around inside the car, and parked next to Tucker's beat-up Bronco.

He turned off the car and got out, leaving the keys dangling in the ignition. He then made his way up the trailer's cinder block steps and knocked one, two, three times before Darlene came to the door with Tobias thrown over her shoulder. She patted his back, attempting to burp him, stopping every so often to rub the area where she patted him.

"Tuck, the bastard is here," she yelled the words to the space of the trailer behind her. Rawlins rolled his eyes. A few moments later, Tucker emerged from the hallway carrying a tin of chew. He removed the lid, took a pinch, stuffed it in his lower lip, then recapped it and jammed it in his jacket pocket.

"What's all the fuss? And what did I tell you about contacting me on the phone?" Rawlins asked, frustration and annoyance evident in his voice. He closed the door behind him and stepped further inside the trailer. Darlene paced the small living area with Tobias held against her shoulder.

"This shit can't wait, Lou."

"What can't wait?"

Tucker looked at Darlene with eyes that begged her to leave the room.

"I think we're past that point," Darlene said, laying Tobias gently down on the couch and wrapping him in a blanket.

"Wilma."

"Jennings?"

"Yeah. She came by here asking where BoDeen was."

"And what did you tell her?"

"That I didn't know where he was," Tucker said. "That we scattered after the place went up and I haven't seen him since."

"Did she buy it?"

"Fuck no she didn't. She was ranting about finding out what happened, and she isn't going to let up either."

"She's a piece of work, that woman," Darlene said from the couch.

Tucker could see Rawlins' thoughts reeling. This was getting out of hand. One thing led to another and soon it would be too big to handle and they'd both be sitting in county jail waiting to be sent to the big house.

"What the fuck are we gonna do?" Tucker's voice was shaky, betraying his anxiety over the situation. He wiped the sweat from the slick of his palms on his jeans, then jammed his hands in his pockets to keep them from going epileptic.

"Let me think on it for a bit."

"I don't think we have a bit."

"What fuckin' choice have we got? I need to think here, dammit," Rawlins exclaimed. He limped over to a busted up recliner that sat opposite the couch. "And until then, I have a proposition for you." He adjusted his gun belt and sat down on the chair. He stretched out his bad leg and kept it steady with the heel of his boot planted on the floor. "One last thing and we'll end it here."

Tucker and Darlene waited, motionless, for him to continue.

"This man, Finch McAllister, the one who pulled the gun on himself the other night," Rawlins said. He shifted to peer around Tucker, who was standing between him and Darlene, to get a glimpse of her face. "You know who I'm talking about."

"Wait, what?" Tucker's attention was immediately diverted from Rawlins as he turned to look at Darlene.

"I didn't tell you, but some john pulled a gun the other night while I was working."

"And you didn't think to tell me? For Christ's sake."

"Other things came up, Tuck."

"That doesn't matter," Rawlins said, interrupting before it escalated into an argument. "What matters is that the gun he pulled was stolen from me and I want it back."

"Is it really that important?" Tucker asked, his hands were at his sides again and he ran his fingers along his palms.

"It belonged to my father, so yes, I'd say it is pretty damn important."

Tucker tugged at the AA chip he had hung around his neck. He understood the importance of something like that. The property of dead men is holy and sometimes the only way to let others know they were here at all.

"Okay, and what is the proposition?"

"You get the gun back and we call it quits. Everything. No more cooking, no more splitting profit, all done. We go our separate ways."

"Who is this guy in possession of it now?"

Tobias began to fuss. Darlene picked him up, laid him on her lap, and bounced her knee to soothe him.

"Name is Finch. Comes from a long line of cat creepers and thieves," Rawlins began explaining. "You've probably heard stories over the years. Going back generations, the whole family was notorious for ripping off drug dealers and other thieves. They were the best at what they did. No one ever dropped a dime on them, nor could anyone catch them in the act. His brother is Colm McAllister. He went a little mad a few years ago and offed a family of five over in Dayton County. He's in Briar Penitentiary right now, scheduled to be executed in a few days.

"I fuckin' knew he looked familiar," Darlene said.

"That would be why. His brother's face is all over the news and plastered across every newspaper."

"Why didn't you tell me all this when I told you about the gun?" Darlene asked.

"I wanted to make sure it was him first."

"And is it?"

"I'm here offering Tucker a way out, aren't I?"

"How can you be sure that it is in fact this guy?" Tucker asked.

"Had a hunch so I drove by The Blue Sparrow and spotted his Impala in the lot. It was his father's car and, from the looks of it, his father must be rolling over in his grave," Rawlins said. "It's him for sure."

"And how do you propose I do this? I can't exactly stroll up and ask him for it back."

"That's your problem. You figure that out and I'll take care of Wilma."

"And if he decides not to do it?" Darlene asked.

"Well, then I haul him in. He can take the fall for everything."

"That's a scumbag thing to do even for you, Lou," she snapped. She looked up at Tucker and said, "This whole situation is out of control and shady as fuck."

"Oh, you mean the situation that you're not even a part of," Rawlins said.

"If it involves Tucker, it involves me."

"You know, maybe if you helped out with Mom I wouldn't need to take as much a cut as I have been. You're not exactly living up to your namesake, Darlene."

"Oh, okay, so this is my fault? You shouldn't be taking anything from us in the first place."

"Let's not go there."

"Meaning?"

"Meaning you two shouldn't have been cooking and selling drugs from the get-go. We're all players here, Darlene. Not a single one of us is innocent of anything."

"Oh, so now I am involved?"

"Enough," Tucker said, stepping between Rawlins and Darlene and putting his hands out. "Enough with this shit. The bickering between you two is starting to become a real pain in the ass."

"Yeah, well tell Little-Ho-Peep over there to shut her cocksucker where it doesn't concern her," Rawlins said.

Tucker ran his hands over his face, knowing the war between the two wasn't going to end until one of them was dead.

"You're disgusting," Darlene said. She looked up at Tucker and said, "And you, you don't even stick up for me."

Tucker was at the end of his rope. He threw his head back and yelled, "I don't because he's not wrong!"

Immediate silence filled the trailer. Rawlins kept his gaze on the floor, trying to stop the slight smirk that was crawling across his face. Darlene threw herself back against the couch, her eyes becoming wet. She blew a stray piece of hair from her face and said, "Is that so?"

"I'm sorry, Darlene," Tucker said as he approached her. He squatted down to meet her eyes, "But your brother is right. It's time to get our shit together. It's time for you to stop whoring and for me to stop slinging crystal. Fuckin' perpetuating these people's mental illness, feeding into their addictions. It's not what I want. I don't want it for us, and I don't want it for Tobias. I'm tired of being a contributing factor and I'm tired of living like this. It hasn't done anything to serve us; it only drags us further into a hole." Tucker stood and turned to face Rawlins. "You too," he said. "You hear me? I'm done. I'm done cooking and I'm done living stuck under your boot. I'll do what you're asking, but then it's over. Darlene and me and Tobias are getting as far away from this hell hole as possible because if I don't, I'm gonna end up like my father and in that madness, there's no telling who I'll take with me."

/ / /

Rawlins left Tucker and Darlene blaming and cursing one another in the confined space of the trailer and headed back to the office to take care of some official business. Once there, he learned that Wilma Jennings had been in to file a missing person's report on BoDeen Carlson. Deputy Plank needed both his vocal and written consent on some lingering police work, after which

Rawlins broke for lunch and swung by his house to check on Lynette.

When Rawlins entered the house, Lucinda was feeding his mother oatmeal, no longer with fruit as she was having trouble swallowing. Poor woman, Rawlins thought. She used to make a mean pot roast every Sunday night with caramelized onions, carrots, mashed potatoes, and fresh biscuits and now she was forced to eat food you didn't have to chew to swallow. She was left on a steady diet of baby food, oatmeal, and pudding. He hated having to look at her in that condition, his heart a little bit heavier every day as she neared the end.

Lynette sat in a rocking chair in the corner of the living room next toa window that looked out over an outside corner of the house where the sunflowers would bloom as tall as men in spring. She was a frail puppet, propped up in a sad display of what she used to be, food sliding down her chin. He told Lucinda to take a break and finished feeding her.

When he was done, he kissed her on the forehead and whispered, "Momma, I'm in a bad way and I think it's going to get worse. I don't know if I'm gonna be around much longer to take care of you. Either the bills or the actions are gonna pull us apart and I don't know what I'm gonna do if that happens. I wanted to be strong the way I watched you be, lifting all the shit the world hurled at you after Dad died." He sighed. "Somewhere along the way, I lost sight of the difference between being tough and being greedy. Not for money, but for not wanting to let you go, and because of that I've been breaking all the rules I told myself I would help keep in place. The same rules that Dad helped keep in place." He put his hand on hers. She felt waxy and cold to the touch. He could feel her knuckle bones through her skin, all the warmth of motherly love emptied out of her because she didn't know who she was, where she was, or who she was supposed to be giving love to anymore. "I guess what I'm trying to say is that I love you and I'm sorry for whatever comes next." He kissed her again and then he left, hurrying past Lucinda, trying to conceal his tears and the fact that he was dying on the inside.

/ / /

By the time Rawlins pulled into Sandy Hills, the low-income housing unit, the sun was a sliver between two mountains and everything was awash in a dull amber hue. There were three rectangular buildings, all structured the same, each with three floors, which meant only one thing. This complex housed a lot of lost souls. He'd heard a rumor that there was an upcoming bill to propose expanding Sandy Hills or building another low-income complex in another location. Fulton was already full of the unemployed and Rawlins thought that adding more units would only encourage more to come. The county was already loose with government benefits. All sorts of people crawled out of the woodwork to collect, not having to do much in return. Simply existing was the only real requirement these days.

He parked the cruiser outside apartment 4A, next to a beat-up blue Toyota, and slunk from the driver's seat and up the front path where he rang a doorbell that was labeled CARLSON/JENNINGS. After a few moments, he forwent the bell and knocked on the door with a fist. When it opened, Rawlins was met with Wilma Jennings. She stood slumped in a loosely wrapped bathrobe with one breast nearly ready to fall out. Her eyes were swollen from crying. Her hair was a rat's nest of tangles, and the skin on her face seemed gray and as thin and dry as rice paper.

"Offering curbside assistance now, Lou?" A cigarette dangled from her lips, and she squinted against a stream of smoke floating into her face.

"May I come in, Wilma?"

She didn't respond. She just walked away, leaving the front door open behind her. Rawlins followed her in. He did a scope of the place, moving only his eyes, and stood trying to breathe through his mouth. The place was foul, the smell like days-old trash and body odor mixed together. The curtains were drawn, and it took a moment for Rawlins' eyes to adjust to the darkness of the apartment. When they finally did, he wished they hadn't. Plates of food and garbage were strewn across a coffee table. The carpet looked as if it hadn't been vacuumed in a decade. Crumpled up clothes were thrown over every surface. Crushed beer and soda cans, socks, and balled-up newspapers were thrown across the floors. The ashtrays overflowed, cigarette ash peppering the end tables that stood beside the couch.

Wilma continued to walk further into the apartment and Rawlins, passing the mess, followed her into a kitchen where the sight didn't get any better. The sink was stuffed with dishes, food stuck to their surfaces. The counters were full of empty containers and cereal boxes and tiny pieces of tinfoil that no doubt held contraband at one point but were now licked clean. She sat at the kitchen table and finished her cigarette without saying a word. She appeared much calmer than how Tucker had described her. Under the overhead light of the kitchen, it became apparent why. Rawlins leaned on the doorjamb and looked at Wilma. She seemed to be focused on something not in the room and her eyes were crystalline glass and heavy. She was doped out of her head. Rawlins clapped his hands to get her attention and her head snapped in his direction.

"Why are you here, Lou?" she asked.

"Checking in on you," he answered. "Standard procedure. Heard you were down at the station to file a report about BoDeen."

"Yeah. He hasn't been home since yesterday."

"Have you checked with his parents?"

"No point," she said, shaking her head. "They haven't spoken to us in months."

"And what time did you last see him yesterday?" Rawlins asked, playing along. He knew that asking the standard questions one would ask when looking into a missing persons case would help him feel out the situation.

"I don't remember the exact time, but sometime in the afternoon. Maybe." Her voice came out in a low, long drawl, her tongue stumbling over the words.

"And you have no idea where he could be?"

"None, but I think that Tucker knows and he ain't talkin'. Was up at his place earlier and I could tell he was playing dumb," she said, tonguing a bad tooth in the back of her mouth.

"What makes you say that?"

"Just a feeling," she said, reaching for a now empty pack of cigarettes. She looked up at Rawlins. "Shouldn't you be writing this down or something?"

"It's all up here," Rawlins said, tapping on his temple with his index finger.

"I'm sure. Or you're just gonna dismiss this whole thing."

"Now why would I do that, Wilma?" Rawlins asked, his voice tinged with sarcasm.

"Because of who BoDeen is."

"And who might that be?"

"Cut the shit. You know exactly who he is and what he does, it ain't no secret."

"Well alright. I'm gonna get going, but I'll get in touch if and when I find something out."

Rawlins turned to leave, and Wilma spoke at his back. "I never did like you, Sheriff," she said. "Even when we was kids. Something about you always rubbed me the wrong way."

The words stopped him, and he turned back around to face Wilma from the doorway of the kitchen. "I don't think you wanna go there," he said.

"Go where, exactly? The truth?"

"You're trash, Wilma. Always have been, always will be. You go through life like you're taking a shit. A forty-seven-year-old woman bedding down with a twenty-three-year-old meth dealer. Good job on the life choices," he said, clapping his hands.

"You son of bitch, get out of my house."

"Gladly."

"And don't think I don't know what you're up to," Wilma added, watching Rawlins' face go slack. "The things you've been involved with. Tucker may not have been upfront with BoDeen, but BoDeen had an idea and that look on your face is saying it's true. It's a good thing your daddy died when he did so he didn't have to see the man his son became. Hiding behind the badge while busting people just as corrupt as him."

The words were a blood rush to his ears. He stepped passsed the threshold and into the kitchen, frustration, anger, and worry boiling through his insides, settling in his guts and heart like molten lead.

"You know, I'd be real fuckin' careful about the next words that come out of your mouth," he said.

"Or what?"

"Or I'll haul your ass down to the station."

"Under what pretense, Sherriff?" she asked, avoiding using his name in an attempt to dehumanize him.

Rawlins scanned the kitchen with his eyes. "I'm sure I'll have no trouble finding something in this drug den you call a home."

"Oh, fuck you. Do it then. I'll sue you and the whole department over false imprisonment and while I'm down there, I'll have a little chat about what you've been up to," she threatened. "I know BoDeen didn't just take off."

Rawlins didn't reply. He didn't even think. An arcane instinct kicked in and he rushed Wilma, picking her up by the neck and lifting her off the chair. He slammed her into the counter and pressed his forearm into her throat. She looked at him, her eyes panicked and stitched to her forehead as she struggled to breathe.

"I warned you to choose your words carefully, you stupid fuckin' cunt. You have no one but yourself to blame for this."

He spun her around and got her neck in the crook of his elbow, applying pressure. She threw her arms up behind her and attempted to claw at his face, but he dodged it, leaning his head back and keeping his arms locked around her neck. She flailed and kicked, gasping for air as her vision began to blur at the edges.

Rawlins put his mouth to her ear and whispered, "You're right. BoDeen didn't run off, although he should have to get away from your tired old ass. He's dead, Wilma, and I sank his ass to the bottom of Catalonia Lake."

Wilma let herself go limp and leaned into Rawlins' chokehold. She threw her feet onto the lip of the counter and pushed off with her legs, sending them both backward and into the kitchen table where they both rolled over the top and crashed onto the floor with a thud. Immense pain punched at Rawlins' knee as he scrambled to regain footing, pushing himself up from the place where he came to rest. Wilma was laid out on her back, sucking lungfuls of air, her vision starting to come back into focus.

Rawlins felt winded as he stood and he stumbled backwards over the mess on the kitchen floor. He reached out with one hand and gripped the counter to keep himself steady as Wilma began to rise from the spot where she lay. His eyes frantically roamed the countertop, searching for something he could use, and he spotted a paring knife. Its handle peeked out from discarded napkins. He slid it from the counter, gripped it firmly in his fist, and, as Wilma sat up, he rushed her again and stuck his boot on her chest, pinning her to the floor. Their eyes met, but nothing was said. They were way past that point.

Rawlins bent forward and plunged the knife deep into Wilma's neck. He twisted its handle one, two, three times and watched blood bubble up from the wound. Wilma coughed a spatter of dark red, choking on it. Rawlins kept his eyes on hers the whole time and when she was done spitting and coughing, when there was no life left in her eyes, he wiped off the knife handle with a dishrag, but left it stuck in her neck. He walked out of the apartment and to the cruiser with a weight of regret perched on his shoulders, knowing his actions weren't those of the man his mother had raised, but those of the man he'd become due to his mother's affliction.

He leaned into the car and took the radio from the dashboard and said, "Attention all units. We have a possible 187. Suspect is one BoDeen Carlson. Seems he stabbed his girlfriend after a dispute. Send an ambulance to Sandy Hills over on Lafayette. Notify all bordering counties that we have a suspect on the loose. Assume him armed and very dangerous."

12.

"You ever try to drown someone? It's tougher than you might imagine and even harder when a little girl is looking up at you through the water with eyes asking why, a look of confusion and panic on her face. In the end, I couldn't wait out the time it would take, and I thought it quite cruel of me to let her suffer like that. Her lungs must have felt like they were going to burst as she held her breath just a little bit longer, hoping I'd have a change of heart. Hoping I'd let her up for air. So I did her like the rest and shot her in the head. Left her floating face up in the bathtub."

Finch spasmed awake, Colm's voice following him from his dreams and riding his neck as dead breath. The lights were off and the room was a shade of blue-black, the occasional passing car throwing slices of illumination across the faded walls and it took him a few moments to remember where he was. He laid there thinking of Colm's death and then of his own. In the last few years,

Finch felt like he had become a stranger thumbing a ride through his own mind. Dying would simply return him to the nothingness from which he came. He found comfort in that thought. He wanted his head to be a vast expanse of black, far from the endless living and the countless dead that haunted his dreams. In some ways he envied Colm for getting off this Godforsaken plane of existence, shirking all the burdens one was expected to haul to the grave.

"Sometimes love turns violent." His brother's voice again, this time coming from somewhere in the room. What had Colm meant by that? Was his act of violence a deflection from what he'd wanted to do to his own family? In the end, was it the only way to save his own blood from himself?

Finch lay awake and let himself adjust to the strangeness of the room, gradually becoming aware of each part of himself, as if they were separate from one another until he felt his body as a whole. When he felt complete, he rolled from the bed and shook loose all the bad thinking that had settled in his head like mud after a great flood. At some point, it had started raining again while he slept. He sat on the edge of the bed and listened to it fall hard and straight, slapping at the parking lot outside the door.

The clock read 8:44. After eating at Dolly's earlier that morning, he'd returned to his motel room and laid down for what he intended to be a nap. Having gotten no sleep the night before, he slept all day instead, which meant his trip to locate the burnt-out shell of the trailer would have to wait until tomorrow.

He got up, dressed, washed his face, and brushed his teeth. All of it was a chore. Then he checked his cell phone and saw two text messages from his boss. One said that he hoped he was getting through what he was dealing with and that he could take as much time as he needed. The second was a reminder that he had two weeks of paid leave and that if he did need longer, they could work something out. He tossed his phone onto the bed and went to stand by the window, peering through a slit in the curtains and out at the parking lot being hammered by the rain. For a moment he thought he saw a hooded figure up ahead at the entrance of the parking lot where the road met the gravel, but he lost sight of it quickly. Whatever he'd seen, if anything at all, it was now lost somewhere in the downpour.

Maybe it was Colm coming to finish what he'd started, he thought. Maybe it was one of the countless voices in his head taking shape and seeking retribution for the lives lost.

Finch threw on his jacket, deciding he wanted some fresh air. He went outside and sat in a metal chair that had once been painted red but was now stripped of its color, what was left now coming off in flakes. The sidewalk was lined with them – one between every door of the motel – most of them in various states of wear. He closed his eyes and felt the cool autumn air against his flushed face. The slanted roof overhead dumped the rain onto the parking lot, and he watched the runoff forming tiny rivers. They flowed into one another and mapped the uneven terrain, extending further than his eyes allowed him to see.

He hadn't heard the footsteps over the noise of the storm so when a voice came, it startled him.

"You look like him." The voice came from behind him. When he turned to meet the face, he saw it was the Native American girl who ran the front desk of the motel. "A little rougher around the edges," she continued, this time speaking above a whisper, talking over the sound of the falling rain, "but it's clear you two are related. You're the brother they mentioned on the news."

Finch didn't say anything. He just sat there wondering if he should be offended by her comment, then quickly decided he shouldn't. She was only being honest and true honesty was very rare these days. And besides, he was inclined to agree with her. He looked like ten pounds of shit shoved in a two-pound bag.

She stood facing away from the neon vacancy sign out front, which threw off a glow and framed the edges of her body in a beautiful candy red. She held a bottle in her left hand, two clear plastic cups in her right. Holding them up, she said, "You look like you could use a drink."

She dragged one of the other metal chairs along the sidewalk to where Finch was seated, the scraping sound sending goosebumps along Finch's neck and arms, and they sat staring through the rain and into the dark. She poured some of the contents of the bottle into one of the cups and handed it to him before pouring another for herself and placing the bottle at her feet. "Homemade mescal," she said, raising her cup. "Don't know if you like it, but it's all I have. My cousin makes it in his garage on the reservation. I'm not much of a drinker, but once in a while I like to indulge."

"Can't say I've ever had it, but I'm not one to turn down a free drink or company from a lovely looking woman," he said. She smiled at the comment. Finch let his shoulders relax. He'd been afraid the comment would come off as too forward. Then he raised his cup to hers and they both took a swig.

Her skin was a beautiful olive color that made him think of almonds. Her hair was pin-straight and black, but at that moment it was tied back in a ponytail, a few strands falling loose and reaching her cheeks. She wore black leggings and purple rubber rain boots with a fitted sweater that was stretched across her torso.

"I hope I'm not bothering you, but it gets lonely out here and I saw you through the window," she explained, motioning with a hand to the front lobby and the window that looked out at the walkway of doors.

"Well, if it's any consolation, it gets lonely everywhere," he replied. He sipped at the liquid again and winced through his teeth.

She laughed. "Not the best tasting stuff, but a little goes a long way. Just enough to take the edge off. I never eat the worm; I always return the bottles to my cousin with them still in it."

Finch swirled the mescal around in the cup, looked over at her, and said, "Do you offer all of your customers' shots of gasoline?"

She talked through a laugh and said, "Nope, just you." There were a few moments of silence between them, the rain keeping it from getting awkward. "Something about your demeanor, the way you carry yourself told me to introduce myself."

"And are you going to?"

"What?"

"Introduce yourself?"

"Oh, shit," she laughed again, and it was evident to Finch that it was a tick that happened when she was nervous. "My name is Mavis."

"How about that. My name's Finch. It seems we're both named after a kind of bird. If this isn't fate, I don't know what is."

"We can have a child and name her Barn Swallow."

Finch chuckled. "You work fast," he said. "Offer a man one drink and we're already having kids."

"Yeah, well, I'm not getting any younger." She looked down into her cup.

"How'd you end up here, Mavis?"

"Long story, but the gist of it is that my parents were tired of the reservation we lived on, so they hauled ass out of there and took me and my brother with them. My father worked labor, saved up, and bought this place. Now I'm running it. They're old now. My father is sick with cancer and my mother is just too old to do the upkeep and the hours it takes to run this place."

"And your brother?"

"Danny is…" She hesitated for a moment before continuing. "Well, he's in an outreach program for opioid addiction."

"Sorry to hear that."

"Don't be. It's his bed and he's lying in it. No sense in giving him pity when it was his choice in the first place. He thinks he's in a unique situation as if he's the only one with problems which he thinks makes his addiction justified. He uses the fact that he's Native American as an excuse for all his failures. He can't get this because he's Native, or so and so won't give me a chance, and blah blah blah. We all have things we carry, mistakes and regrets and such. Some people definitely have it harder than others but using his heritage as an excuse is just plain lazy and disgraceful and he thinks it frees him of personal responsibility. Everyone has a cross to bear, so to speak." She took another sip from the cup. "And he's not the only one," she continued, "The whole country is full of people like him. Never in my life have I seen more people trying to connect with their ancestors while simultaneously being illiterate to their own accountability and growth."

Finch took another sip and thought of Maggie and Sarah and how Mavis had just unknowingly called him out. She was right though. Everyone has something to schlep around and the only one in his way was himself.

"Sorry," she said. "Didn't mean to get so heavy."

"Don't be. I'm not averse to conversations that mean something."

Finch looked out across the street, and for a brief moment, he thought he saw a flash of light coming from the direction of the gas station. "I have to be honest," he continued. "I suffer from a little of what your brother has. My ex would call it Martyr Syndrome."

"Interesting."

"You know, you have some balls. For lack of better terminology, that is. It's not every day that people approach strangers with such heavy points of topic," he said. "And most strangers certainly aren't the brother of a convicted murderer." Hearing himself refer to Colm as a murderer was like thunder in his ears.

"What's that got to do with anything?"

"Some would say guilty by association," said Finch. "As if there was something I could have done to stop him. Like I knew about the storm brewing inside him and all I had to do was give him just one more hug and it would have turned out differently."

"Some people are assholes."

"That is certainly true."

"I believe in the benefit of the doubt, and by all accounts, you don't seem like a threat, just burdened. Plus, what are the chances that two children from the same family would turn out to be killers?" She leaned forward and placed her cup by the bottle that still sat at her feet, then shifted slightly in the chair to cross her legs. She cocked her head in a way that Finch found charming and adorable. "Is there anything you'd like to get off your mind, Finch?"

He looked out into the rain and noticed the way the neon sign out front lit the drops as they fell. A sigh escaped his chest. "Too much to unload on a stranger, but thanks for the drink, Mavis. Very kind of you." He stood from the chair and handed her the plastic cup, turning for the door to his room.

"My people have a saying," Mavis said, still seated. Finch turned his head to meet her gaze. "The past is a rock. If you hold onto it, you can't swim." She bent forward and placed one cup inside the other before hanging them upside down off the neck of the bottle that held the mescal. She stood from the chair and Finch watched the worm slosh around in the liquid as Mavis reclaimed her balance. "The man who committed this heinous crime is going to pay for it with his own life. You don't have to give them your life too."

Finch nodded knowing it was true but also knowing himself. If he didn't carry it, who would? Someone had to, otherwise, his brother's actions would remain just another senseless act of violence and the lives of his victims would seem pointless. Colm being executed just didn't seem like enough in Finch's mind, which brought him to the question, *Who pays the worst price—the man who committed the crime, or his family who has to go on living with it long after he's gone?* It seemed that sometimes, the family of a murderer got a far harsher sentence.

"Goodnight, Mavis," Finch said.

He pushed open the door and disappeared inside.

13.

Tucker kissed Darlene and Tobias goodbye for the night, left the trailer, and got into his truck where he zipped his army jacket up to his chin. He started the engine and then cupped his hands and breathed into them to get them warm. It was another rainy night, and the nights had begun to grow colder as October neared its end.

Darlene begged him not to go to the motel, told him he didn't know what he was walking into. She said her brother was a low life for giving him an ultimatum such as the one he presented, but Tucker felt like he didn't have a choice. Rawlins was giving him an out and he needed to take it. If he could pull it off, then he was free to leave with Darlene and Tobias. They'd be free to start over and do it right. Rawlins had him in a corner and he knew it. Darlene tried to convince him that her brother was bluffing, but Tucker couldn't chance it. Problem was, he had no plan.

He'd spent the day wracking his brain while crammed under the Bronco, changing the oil, and fine-tuning some things that needed work, but had come up with nothing. He knew very little about the guy he was supposed to be getting this gun back from and he knew even less about his habits. All he had was a description that, at best, resembled a cartoon of a person in his head. He also had a description of the gun, which Tucker supposed was more important than the man who possessed it. The best he could come up with, as he aimed his truck down the dirt driveway, the headlights carving out a tunnel of light through the dark, was to head over to The Blue Swallow Inn, park across the street, and scope out the scene in hopes that something would come to him while he watched and waited for a moment to present itself.

A third of a mile from his destination, he killed the headlights so he wasn't obvious to anyone who may have been outside the motel. He wanted to be as discreet as possible. He steered the Bronco toward the shoulder of the road and crept into the gas station parking lot where he pulled a U-turn and came to a stop, the truck facing the motel across the street. He cut the engine. The lights were off, the gas station closed, and behind it, the church, which stood at the end of a rough and rugged trail flanked by sloping hills of dead and dying grass, was dark and seemingly empty. Pulling into the lot, Tucker had caught a glimpse of it, its fading white paint going to grey then to muted bone. It jutted up from the landscape like a giant toothache under a vast and endless sky crowded with nimbus clouds. It was the church his parents had taken him to as a child to worship God in the company of strangers each Sunday.

Praying is like a bowel movement, Tucker thought. *Intimate and to be performed in a clean, quiet place away from the watchful eyes of others.* And then he thought of the hypocrisy behind his father's final act as images of his parents came to him in rushes of red, filling the space behind his eyes and burning across his brain like a shadow traced in gasoline and set ablaze with a match. He did his best to push it to the deepest end of his skull, that place we all dump the bad shit of our lives and never sort out, always thinking that we have more time, always telling ourselves tomorrow.

He sat awhile in the cab of the Bronco and wrestled with the images of his dead parents, his brain like a spastic viewfinder firing off shots of various angles, wide views, and close-ups, their bodies splayed across the living room floor while he stared through the rain specked windshield at the motel across the street.

How was he going to pull this off?

The inside of the truck smelled vaguely of oil and gasoline, and the dampness stuck in the seats held the scent of cistern water. He cracked the window for fresh air, then draped himself over the steering wheel, a freight train of emotions rolling through his body, his blood pulsing at his temples.

He eyed the Impala that Rawlins had mentioned and remembered Darlene telling him that the man named Finch had pulled the gun in the car. Maybe it could be that simple. Wait for a bit longer, until he felt there was a good opportunity, jimmy open the car door, and find the gun stashed under the seat or in the glove compartment. He'd return it to Rawlins and be free and clear. With the little bit of money he did have saved up, he and Darlene, and Tobias could be on the road and out of Fulton by tomorrow. He could find work as a mechanic or a logger. He could work as a ranch handler or paint houses. He wasn't afraid of hard labor and that opened far more possibilities for him so long as the stigma of what his father had done didn't follow him into the rest of the world like a hungry dog.

Tucker dug the palms of his hands into his eyelids until he saw flecks of light like furious snow descending from a black sky. His jaw ached from clenching his teeth and he opened his mouth a few times to ease the tension. The anticipation of getting it over and done with was worse than not knowing whether he would live or die in the process.

The rain seemed to be letting up, so he slid from the cab of the truck and out into the stillness of the rain-soaked night, his breath visible in puffs of smoke as he exhaled against the cold air. What little rain that did continue to fall felt like drops of lead against the back of his neck. He readjusted the mesh cap on his head and shut the truck door. He walked quietly to the foot of the gas station parking lot, ready to make a break for the Impala, which was parked between rooms eight and nine if his eyesight was correct.

Through the large front window of the check-in area, he watched a young woman mill about from one end of the lobby to the other, performing menial tasks. She wiped down the check-in counter with a rag, collected various magazines, and stacked them neatly on a small table that sat between two chairs. When she was finished with that, she walked behind the counter and began to dust, what looked to be, giant elk or deer antlers that hung off the wall. She turned her back to the window and Tucker readied himself to push off with one foot and start his sprint across the road when he heard a cry of distress coming from behind him in the dark.

His heart was thunderous in his chest and ears as the cries came again, louder this time and more pained. Tucker turned from the road, his eyes sweeping the area in search of the source. He held his breath to try to get a better earful. It came again in clips and bursts, and he realized that it was coming from inside the gas station.

It certainly sounded human. He'd lived his entire life in these woods and had been hunting since he was young. He knew the sound a wounded animal would make, and this wasn't the sound of any wounded animal.

Tucker backed away from the road and made his way to the entrance of the gas station, cautious, but fueled with equal amounts of curiosity.

14.

Abraham lay on the motel bed, his arms outstretched with nothing but a towel haphazardly thrown across his lap. He stared at the ceiling in silence. To Clem, he looked like a black Jesus lost in thought. He stood by the dresser that held a television set and watched Abraham for a moment. The screen flickered with images of war, but no sound came from the speakers. At the foot of the bed was a Sig Sauer P229 Legion Compact and a sawed-off 12-gauge shotgun with a five-round capacity that was packed with five slugs of high-velocity buckshot. Clem walked to the bed, took the 9mm from the mattress, and tucked it into the back of his waistband. He threw on his trench coat and slid the shotgun into a makeshift holster that had been sewn into the inside flaps of the coat itself. He adjusted the collar, pulling it snug against the back of his neck.

"Time to get into character," Clem said.

Abraham looked at him from where he was sprawled out on the bed and said, "You're already a character."

Clem held up his arms in a show of display. "How do I look?" he asked.

"Like a man who just go out of prison and is about to do some real dumb shit," Abraham said, that familiar sinking feeling in the pit of his stomach returning. It was a feeling he always got right before they pulled a job.

"Get up and get dressed," Clem said. "You need to be ready."

Abraham tossed the towel from his lap and got dressed in the same clothes he'd had on earlier that day, after which he moved about the room packing up what little they had so that when the time came, they would be ready for their escape. He placed the bag that contained their belongings on the bed. On top of that, he laid down his Glock 19 for easy access. He'd sit on the edge of the bed and meditate, a practice he'd picked up and taken to in prison, and wait for Clem's return.

They approached one another in the middle of the room, knowing what came next. Clem hooked his hand around the back of Abraham's neck, pulled his face close to his own and they kissed for a few seconds, both getting lost in the moment. Abraham wanted to live there in that moment forever, far away from all the worry and risks.

"See you soon," Clem said, staring into Abraham's eyes and pressing his forehead against his.

"See you soon, you psycho."

Clem made for the door and as he opened it, Abraham said, "Hey, how do you know a bank robber is gay?"

Clem looked over his shoulder and said, "He ties up the safe and blows the guard."

They both smiled and then Clem was gone, out into the parking lot where a wind-laced rain cut sideways angles and pummeled him in the side of the face. He threw up the collar of his coat and pushed against the squall, keeping to the edge of the parking area. When he reached the road, he made a swift break for the gas station across the street.

/ / /

Clem reached the gas station just as the overhead lights to the gas pumps went off. He pushed through the door and into the dimly lit space. All the lights inside were turned off. The only light being offered now was from the beer cooler that sat in the corner. Old Man Hoffstetter was standing with his back to Clem, counting out that day's profits. He turned his head when he heard the bell above the door jingle and was met with the visual of Clem standing there, drenched from the rain, and dripping all over the floor.

Clem cleared his throat. "Hey, sorry about this. I know you're closing and all, but is there any chance I can grab another six-pack? Both me and my buddy passed out earlier, tired from driving all day and such," Clem explained, "and we slept longer than we planned."

The old man turned to face Clem, put his hands flat on the counter, and said, "Well, I'm counting out the register now, but if you make it quick, I don't see why I couldn't do that for ya."

"Thanks," Clem said, faking a sigh of relief. He walked to the cooler and grabbed the sixer, then ping-ponged his way back to the register and placed it on the counter. "I'll make it easy for you," Clem said, digging into his pocket. "I'll give you ten and you can keep the change."

"That won't be necessary, but thanks for the offer."

"I insist. I appreciate it. I know how annoying it can be when customers come in last minute." He slapped a crumpled bill down on the counter. "And one more thing?"

"What's that, kiddo?" Hoffstetter looked up from the crumpled bill and into Clem's eyes, that glossy blue seeming to signal to the old man that something wasn't quite right.

Clem reached into his knee-length coat, pulled out the sawed-off shotgun, and aimed the barrel straight into the old man's chest. "I'll take all the cash you have sitting on the counter there behind your back."

"Ain't this some shit. I should have known better than to trust a twerp like you," Hoffstetter said, keeping his hands flat on the counter.

"Excuse me?"

"You heard me. I called you a twerp. Coming in here pointing a gun at an old man like this. You should be ashamed of yourself."

"I don't want any trouble, old man."

"Says the man with a gun pointed at another."

"Just hand over the cash and I'll be on my way. You don't have to get hurt."

Hoffstetter raised his hands and turned to retrieve the cash from where it had been laid out. It was all separated by bills and the old man scooped up the stacks and asked, "Would you like it in a bag or are you just gonna stuff it all in your pockets like the animal you are?" He turned to face Clem.

"What the hell is with you, old man?"

"I'll tell you what's with me. I've been working all my life. And then people like you run around and take from hardworking, honest people like myself. This whole damn country has gone down the toilet due to lowlifes like you."

"It hardly has anything to do with me. You wanna blame someone, blame your government for making it nearly impossible for people like me to survive. A man's gotta do what a man's gotta do," Clem said, smiling at Hoffstetter. He grabbed the cash the old man had wadded in his arthritic fist. "Now put your hands back on the counter."

The old man did what Clem said. "What a bunch of hogwash," he murmured. "Blaming everyone else for your failures. Fuckin' no good lazy brats."

"You just don't quit, do you? You are truly a piece of work. If I didn't need this money as badly as I do, I'd almost feel bad for doing this because I like you, old man."

"Lucky me."

Clem laughed and stuffed the cash that would fit into his coat pocket. What didn't fit he stuffed into the pocket of his pants, keeping the gun aimed at Hoffstetter.

"Now, how about that church out back?"

"What about it?"

"I'm assuming it has a donation box."

"You no-good sonuvabitch," Hoffstetter said through a dry throat. He lifted his hands off the counter and threw them up toward Clem as if to grab him by the collar of his shirt.

Clem brought the butt of the gun around and busted the old man's face into blood and snot. He nearly went down but caught himself and then lifted his aging body back up straight with the help of the counter.

"Try that again and it'll be bullets."

The old man looked at Clem through watery eyes, blood streaming down his chin.

"Now, time to get moving," Clem said. "And do it slowly." He waved the gun in the direction he wanted Hoffstetter to go. "You're coming with me."

"I ain't got no choice but to do it slowly, you fuckin' nitwit," Hoffstetter said as he rounded the counter to join Clem on the other side. Clem followed his movements with the barrel of the shotgun and laughed at his comment.

"I'm assuming there's a backdoor to this fine establishment."

"Your assumption would be correct."

"Good. You're gonna take the lead and bring me up to that church and once I get what I'm after, I'll be on my way and you're free to go about the rest of your night."

There was no warning. No sound to indicate that someone else was there with them, but out of nowhere, Clem felt a sharp pain in his side as something had punctured his body. As it slid into him, he could feel its sharp edges scrape bone as the object came to rest in his ribcage. He screamed out in pain, his voice like a wounded animal filling the darkness of the store. His finger hit the trigger and shot off a round. Buckshot ripped into Hoffstetter and sent him backward and onto the floor where he yelled out in agonizing pain, his chest and stomach peppered with gaping wounds and powder burns. In an instinctual reaction and without looking, Clem threw his elbow up behind him where it made contact with a face. He heard the snap of cartilage and when he spun around to get a look, he saw it was a woman. She was bent over cupping her nose, blood running between her fingers.

"Who the fuck are you?" Clem swung the gun up in her direction and almost went down from the pain barreling through his side. He managed to keep his composure and winced through his teeth, his anger keeping him on his feet more than anything else at that moment.

The woman, still hunched over, had moved her hand from her nose to her mouth to stifle cries as she looked to the floor and saw the old man lying in a pool of blood.

He twitched and writhed, uncontrollable moans escaping his throat.

Clem reached for his side, the spot where the pain was permeating from, and felt the handle of a knife protruding from his ribs. "What the fuck did you do?" His voice was laced with exasperation and confusion.

"Only the same thing you done to my father," the woman said through her fingers. "You fuckin' killed him." Her breathing became more labored as she struggled to suck in air.

"Believe me, that wasn't my intention. In fact, you only got yourself to blame for that," Clem said. He bit his lower lip, attempting to deflect the pain pumping itself from the puncture wound. It was pointless. He tasted blood. "And despite this little hiccup, we're gonna finish what I came here to do."

/ / /

Outside, the moon was obscured by clouds, but its glow bled through and created a halo effect that hung high in the night sky as the woman led Clem out the back door and down the trail that led to the church, the barrel of the shotgun planted firmly in her back. When they reached the church, the woman pushed through the front doors and into the dank space that was lined with pews on either side. The air smelled of mildew and something like wet hay with the slight hint of pine buried underneath it all.

"It's in the backroom," the woman said, pointing to the furthest end of the building. Her nose had stopped bleeding, but it was starting to swell. She reached up every so often to tenderly feel her face, receiving a pulse of pain at the slightest touch.

"This thing has really got an ass on her," Clem said. "From the outside, she doesn't look like much, but now that we're in here she really opens up. In the dark, it seems like it goes on forever." He nudged the woman with the shotgun to keep moving. They walked the aisle between the pews, turned left at the pulpit where a life-size Jesus hung on the wall above it. Clem was always spooked by the crucifixion. He found it ghostly, strange, and just plain hypocritical that anyone would worship such a barbaric image while decrying the violence inflicted on others in the modern world.

Once in the back, the woman reached for a light switch that was on the wall, illuminating the place with the flick of her wrist. There was a desk pushed into a corner. Cardboard boxes, papers spilling over their lips, lined the opposite wall. Plastic figures of the Virgin Mary, Jesus, and various saints in praying positions were scattered throughout the area, some face down, others stacked haphazardly against the walls. Dust and cobwebs crowded the corners. Spots of black mold spattered the sheetrock, looking like a connect the dots picture puzzle waiting to be finished.

"Haven't you people ever heard the saying 'Cleanliness is next to Godliness'?"

The woman didn't answer at first. She walked to the desk, took a metal box from a drawer, and held it out for Clem to take. "That's not what it means," she said.

"Excuse me?"

"The saying you just quoted. It's not what you think it means nor is it actually from the Bible."

"Well, it should be. That book has been rewritten more times than anyone can count, that saying should be incorporated. Teach people about being neat and clean. I've never seen such an ungodly mess in such a holy place," Clem retorted. He coughed, the harsh smell of rot and mold filling his lungs as the pain came again from where he'd been punctured in his side. "I've been in prisons cleaner than this."

The woman stood, still holding the donation box, but Clem didn't take it. He just waved the gun at her and they retraced their steps out of the room and back out into the nave where Clem propped himself up on a pew. He directed the woman to do the same. He sat for a few moments, breathing through the discomfort. He was beginning to feel woozy from the blood loss.

"What are we doing?" the woman asked. The box rested in her lap and she nervously tapped the top with her fingernails.

"I need to sit for a minute," Clem explained as if it weren't obvious. "If you haven't noticed, you fucked me up pretty good, lady."

"Yeah, well, you killed my father," she said, her eyes growing wet again.

"As I said, that wasn't my intention. Your little act of heroism back there is what did him in. Surprising a man with a gun," he scoffed. "I only wanted the money." Clem shifted and sat slumped against the back of the pew, gun resting on his leg, still pointed at the woman. "Don't get me wrong, I don't blame you. People resort to violence because our moral code demands it. It is necessary to our survival."

"I don't believe that.

"Don't or refuse?"

"What's the difference?"

"Not believing something because you truly don't is worlds apart from knowing it to be true but refusing to accept it." He shifted again, this time sitting straight up, trying to find a comfortable position. "Violence is necessary and without it, we wouldn't be here in the first place. The Big Bang was an act of violence. A collection of molecules and atoms and gasses converge then explode resulting in organisms that eventually developed into humans, the same men and women who carried on the tradition by copulating. Your father penetrating your mother and spasming a cluster of seeds which resulted in you, a baby who would violently cry to let her mother know she needed to be fed."

The woman glanced up at the crucifix and Clem followed her line of vision. Jesus stretched out along the cross, his loincloth looking as if it were ready to fall away. Clem thought of Abraham laid out across the bed back at the motel.

"Take your boy up there," Clem said, motioning to the giant Jesus with a bloody finger. "He wasn't much before being nailed to that thing. He wandered around spitting some early version of jailhouse philosophy, hanging out with the derelicts and whores. Not a bad life by any means, but not all that different from my own. It wasn't until he was reborn through an act of *violence* that he transcended and truly became the savior to millions. So yeah, violence is necessary to our survival as it was the thing that put us here in the first place." He turned his eyes back to her and they met each other's gaze. "Which brings us to our current situation."

The woman blinked and wiped tears from her face.

"I think we can agree that both our unexpected presences put a bit of a nail in either of our plans. If I don't kill you here, as in right now, you'll call the cops and give a description and that'll be the end of me because I'm not going back to prison. But if I end your life, right here, right now, I can walk away free and clear. Do you agree that your death is necessary to my survival?" Clem asked.

A sudden silence filled the church. The woman could hear her heart trying to pump its way out of her chest. She swallowed hard, her mouth like sandpaper, and asked, "So are you? Going to kill me that is?"

"That's what I'm trying to decide." Clem pushed himself from the pew and stood in front of the woman. "Tell you what," Clem pulled a cigarette from his pocket, lit it, and sucked back a deep drag, the puncture wound throwing out pain as his lungs expanded to take in the smoke. "I'll give you however long it takes me to smoke this cigarette to pray to your God and if he comes down and stops me, then it was meant to be, and you can walk away. If he doesn't, then you'll die knowing your God abandoned you in the time you needed him most."

She began to pray in whispers, her eyes shut tight. Clem watched her lips for a moment, then decided to let her have her privacy and wandered over to the pulpit where he paced and smoked, the knife still protruding from his side and the shotgun resting on his shoulder. His skin was clammy, and he wiped the sweat from his forehead with the sleeve of his coat, knowing the color had drained from his face. He was starting to feel the effects of the stab wound, the adrenaline that had kept him going up until this point starting to dwindle. He knew he was going to need a doctor, but he also knew that just wasn't in the cards.

He stopped pacing and held himself up with a hand against the pulpit, looking over his shoulder at the woman whose eyes were still firmly shut, her lips furiously moving. He sucked back the last few drags of his cigarette and threw it to the church floor. "Times up, lady," he said.

He walked to where she sat. Her eyes were now wide open and begging him as she looked up at Clem approaching. He took the box from her lap, held the gun to her face, and said, "I guess God is on your side. It's not your time." He stepped back from her and saw a look of elation flood her features, as she realized she was going to live. "You're going to give me a head start, after which you do whatever you feel it is you need to do."

She nodded and Clem lowered the shotgun.

"I'm truly sorry about your father. He seemed like a decent man. And if it's worth anything, I have more respect for a person with your kind of faith than I do the so-called 'deathbed believers' you come across in prison. Those guys take the cake. Claiming they've changed their ways, suddenly becoming enlightened with no real way to test their supposed and sudden faith. Sure it's easy to say that when you're locked up for twenty hours a day and there's no pussy or liquor or the possibility of a big score hanging in front of your face. I don't buy it. Ain't nothin' gonna save their souls, if they even have one to begin with. But you, you've always believed and go on believing through sheer faith. And though I may not agree with you, I can't argue that kind of commitment."

He turned to go but stopped and wavered on his feet, the loss of blood making him dizzy again. He could feel wetness soaking through his shirt and the escape of liquid out around the hilt of the knife. He hung his head and spoke, this time without looking at her. "What's your name?" he asked.

"I don't think that's appropriate," she said, sitting with her hands on her lap where the box had been, looking up at the crucifix.

"Maybe not, but I think it's necessary."

"You killed my father and I'd rather not give you any more power over me. We made it this far, why go and make it worse? I don't want to know your name. I don't need to carry the name of the man who took the only thing I had left in the world. It would only haunt me for the rest of my life."

"That's exactly why I need to know yours."

The woman swallowed and said, "Brooklynn. With two n's."

Clem nodded his head and walked the aisle between the pews. At his back, he heard Brooklynn begin to pray again in whispers, this time no doubt praying for his death.

Two prayers answered in one night, Clem thought. *Maybe there is a God.*

He pulled open the church doors, the echo of them closing filling the hallowed space inside as he forced himself back in the direction of the motel.

15.

All the lights were off, but the door was unlocked. Tucker entered the filling station, following the pained screams that seemed to be drifting on the damp wind. Once inside, he stood for a moment, letting his eyes adjust to the dark, and when they finally did, he saw a pair of legs splayed across the floor, lit only by the bulb of a beer cooler. He rushed to the old man lying in a pool of blood. He was on his back, his stomach and chest shot to Swiss cheese by what Tucker guessed was a shotgun. The old man coughed and choked on his own fluids.

Tucker had known Old Man Hoffstetter his whole life. He'd been running the store for as long as Tucker had been alive and headed the church services as far back as Tucker could remember. As he knelt by his side, his knees sliding in the old man's blood, he was bum rushed with a sudden feeling of melancholy and regret. Whose regret, he didn't know. His own, perhaps. The sight of violence reminded him of what could end up being the outcome of his own life. Up until a couple of days ago, he'd always been able to escape the violence that usually accompanied dealing drugs but starting with BoDeen it seemed he was being hurled in a direction that would end no differently than the old man, whose body was starting to let go of what little it had left. Or maybe it was regret in knowing that he deserved it and that the old man didn't. Or maybe he was feeling the old man's regret as he looked into his eyes rimmed with deep wrinkles and saw life slipping off to some unknown place, an unfinished task he thought he had a bit more time to complete weighing on his conscience. It's hard to tell when you're that close to someone as they're dying, regardless of if you know them well, just a little bit, or not at all. There's a sort of bond that other relationships could never understand, only made more intense if you're looking them in the eyes as they're doing it.

Whatever the feeling was, it was suddenly replaced by the feeling of Hoffstetter's hand on Tucker's knee and the sounds of his voice escaping a bruised throat.

"He has my daughter. He has Brooklynn. You need to call the cops," Hoffstetter said through a blood-filled throat.

"Who has her?"

"I don't know who he is but it's the same man who riddled me with buckshot. Stopped in earlier this morning with another fella who was colored. They drove a grey Plymouth. That much I know." He coughed and choked and coughed some more, blood erupting from his mouth and onto his face.

Tucker recalled seeing a Plymouth parked in the motel parking lot across the street.

"I'll have to go back out to my truck," Tucker said. "I left the cell phone there."

"Never mind that. There's a phone over by the register," Hoffstetter said. He tried to point in the direction of the phone, but he had nothing left in the way of energy and his arm just twitched and flopped around in the blood spilling from his body like a fish spasming in a puddle of water.

In a knee-jerk reaction, Tucker hurdled Hoffstetter's body and landed on the other side, nearly losing his footing. He almost went down in the blood, areas already starting to coagulate and become thick like syrup. Tucker could feel it on the bottoms of his boots as he walked through it slowly to keep himself from sliding. He felt like a fly stuck to flypaper. When he reached the register, he yanked the phone off the receiver and began dialing 911 before he thought better of it and stopped himself. To his own horror, he began to justify letting the old man bleed out and leaving his daughter's life in the hands of fate.

I can't have the cops swarming this place. It'll blow my chances of getting the gun and starting over, clean. Not to mention the repercussions from Rawlins. He's old. Even without the wounds, he has what, a couple of years left in him? Should you sacrifice the rest of your own life and the lives of

Darlene and Tobias for a woman you hardly know and a man who would be dead soon from old age anyway?

If the stakes are high enough a man can justify, to himself, anything he does.

He set the phone back on the receiver and walked back to the old man whose breathing had now become more labored as he struggled to hold onto life a little bit longer.

"I can't have the cops here," Tucker said, squatting next to the old man who at one point in Tucker's life had sold him bait and given him tips on fishing when Tucker was just a boy.

"What?"

"I'm sorry, sir."

"What are you up to, boy?"

"Nothing good, I can tell you that," Tucker said, "but none of it has anything to do with you or your own. Best I can do is try to make you more comfortable, before...you know..."

"You're going to burn for this."

"Maybe so, but it couldn't be any worse than the hell I'm already living, one I won't be able to escape if the cops show up."

Hoffstetter said nothing. He jerked and coughed up the blood filling his lungs one last time and then he was limp, a faraway look in his eyes. Tucker removed his mesh cap, let his head hang limp on his neck, and said a prayer for the old man before going to find a tarp in the backroom to cover the body. When it was over, he retreated out to the parking lot and across the street to The Blue Swallow Inn.

16.

The 64 ragtop Impala was unlocked, something Tucker found out when he lifted the handle to the passenger side door and it popped open with no resistance. There was a slight squeak to the metal and Tucker stopped dead in his tracks. He looked toward the doors of the motel and around the dimly lit parking lot to make sure the sound hadn't given him away. When he felt the coast was clear, he proceeded with caution with bated breath, and his heart pounding in his chest, ears, and throat.

He slid across the leather interior and closed the door, leaving it slightly ajar for an easy escape, if it came to that. He kept low so that any potential passersby wouldn't see him through the windows. He did a sweep under the seats with his hand, but came up empty of the gun, instead getting fistfuls of fast-food wrappers, used napkins, and various crumpled up papers. He eased himself up from the seat, peeking over the dashboard, his asshole cinched tight at the thought of someone spotting him inside the car. He popped open the glove compartment and staring him in the face was his ticket out. A .36 snub-nosed revolver with a wooden handle, decorated with the symbol Rawlins had talked about.

He lifted the gun from its spot, felt the weight of it in his hand, and opened the cylinder. One bullet rested in a chamber. Tucker dug at the junk in the glove compartment in hopes of finding the other bullets. He came up with one and chambered it, then found two more tucked into the folds of the seat at his back and did the same with them. He snapped the cylinder shut and began sliding across the seat on his back, legs first out the door.

/ / /

Mavis watched a figure she thought to be a man through the large window of the motel office as it crossed the parking lot and ducked behind the 64 Impala that she knew belonged to Finch McAllister. Moments later, the passenger side door opened, and the shadow seemed to slide inside, moving about the interior. The lighting was bad with only the neon sign out front and the dim bulbs set into the angled roof above the motel doors. It wasn't enough to get a better look. That, and she *was* watching through a window fifty feet from the action that was taking place. She'd needed glasses for a while, and it was moments like this that reminded her of that.

She didn't know what it was, but there was something about the man in room eight that made her heart skip a beat. That stupid feeling could not be explained without sounding like a thirteen-year-old girl. She was lonely, that wasn't a secret. How could she not be? Stuck out in the middle of nowhere, forced to run a business she couldn't care less about, and surrounded by locals who were just as rough looking as they were ignorant would force anyone to avoid socializing. It was rare, but when men like Finch passed through, it was a relief. She thought him to be handsome, in a rugged way, and the fact that he was the brother of a man who would soon be put to death added a level of mystery that only intrigued her more. She was a fan of true crime, like so many people nowadays, and she spent most of her time consuming anything crime-related through books, documentaries, and her favorite, podcasts. And now a guest was staying in her motel that had lived through something she had only read or heard about and, being as good looking as he was, she just wanted to throw herself at him. Their meeting earlier had not gone as planned and she felt a little foolish for being so forward, but the few flirtatious comments he had made brought a smile to her face and filled her chest with the kind of excitement she hadn't felt since her early days at college where she'd studied criminology. But those dreams had ended when she was burdened with the task of taking care of the family business so her mother could take care of her dying father. She told herself it was only temporary so she could get through the monotony of day-to-day life out in the boonies. And she hoped that was true.

Mavis watched the figure a bit longer, then left the window and went behind the office desk where she picked up the receiver of the landline phone and dialed out.

/ / /

The phone rang three times before Finch picked it up. The bedside radio was on and music drifted through the room as he rolled over to the opposite side of the bed and picked up the receiver. He couldn't for the life of him think of who it could be. No one knew that he was staying at the motel and anyone that would want to contact him would have called his cell phone.

"Hello?"

"Hi, Finch, this is Mavis at the front desk. Sorry to disturb you, but there's someone out front going through your car..."

Finch didn't respond. He didn't even let her finish speaking. He dropped the receiver where it rolled off the table, hanging just short of the floor by its coiled cord, and launched himself off the bed. He landed against the door with a thud and threw it open, stepping out into the parking lot to see what Mavis was talking about. A man was hunched down in the front seat of his car. He approached quietly and rounded the front end to the passenger side door.

/ / /

The pain started at Tucker's knees, then bullet-trained its way up his body and echoed in his head as the passenger door was opened and then slammed shut on his legs, followed by a hostile voice that asked, "Who the fuck are you and what are you doing in my car?"

A pained scream escaped Tucker's chest. He didn't even realize the sound came from him at first.

Through the window, Tucker saw a man who he could only assume was Finch. He was caught red-handed, and he wasn't going to blame the guy for acting out in his own defense. But it wasn't going to stop Tucker from defending himself either. He tucked his legs back into the car, ignoring the pain, and put his feet up against the door paneling and when Finch came again, he threw the door open with his feet, knocking Finch to the parking lot gravel.

Tucker slid from the car like jelly, fumbled a moment to gain a stance, and lifted the gun. He pointed it at Finch, who was also fumbling to stand. The sight of the gun stopped Finch in his tracks.

"You gonna shoot me with my own gun?"

"Not your gun, partner."

They stood in the cold dark of the parking lot, their breath steaming from their mouths in puffs of smoke that floated upward and dissipated somewhere above them.

Finch nodded. "That remains to be seen."

"And so it does, but since you're the one that's unarmed in this situation and seeing that I got you dead bang, we'll say it's already come to pass."

"And what, you escape with that newly formed limp?"

"Yeah, about that," Tucker said. "I should cap you in the knee. Even out the score."

"That would hardly be even. I'd owe you one."

Mavis approached in their periphery, nearly spooking Tucker into pulling the trigger. He swung his arm in her direction and kept the gun locked on her for a few moments before swinging it back in the direction of Finch, who had taken a step forward, hoping to advance on Tucker while he was distracted.

Mavis's body hiccupped at the sight of the revolver, suddenly realizing the severity of the situation.

Tucker's eyes moved from Mavis to Finch.

"Keep the gun on me," Finch said.

"That was my plan."

Mavis eyed Finch and asked, "Should I have called the cops?"

Tucker and Finch answered in unison. "No."

"We don't need to involve him," Finch said. "Do we?" He looked at Tucker and their eyes locked. "He's caused enough of a mess, so just lower the gun and we can talk this shit out. Whatever he's up to, he has you involved in a situation you clearly don't want to be in."

Tucker felt a mental pull from either direction. He knew that no matter the decision he made, he'd be moving as much away from something as he was toward something and that neither outcome was guaranteed or even necessarily wanted.

He lowered the gun.

"Good, this is good. Now let's go inside and figure this out."

"I'm not going anywhere," Tucker said. "We're gonna stay exactly where we are."

"I'd rather not have this conversation in the parking lot."

"Well, then no deal." Tucker raised the gun again in Finch's direction.

"Okay, okay," Finch said, putting his hands up.

Tucker lowered the gun again, and, keeping his eyes on Finch, rubbed at his knees. They were already starting to stiffen, no doubt due in part to the damp air. He was regretting parking across the street. He wanted to haul ass out of there, but the pain in his legs wouldn't allow the distance he needed to cover to get back to the Bronco.

"I just came here for the gun. I didn't intend for all this," Tucker said, hunched over and kneading at his legs.

"Fair enough, but I can't let you leave here with it," Finch said. "It's just not an option."

"Just let him have it back and whatever is going on between you two will be over and done with."

Finch almost laughed. "It's not that simple and you know it."

"It rarely is with him."

"Exactly." Finch relaxed his shoulders.

Keeping that gun had become less about his own selfish motives and more about ensuring that Rawlins didn't get the satisfaction of winning. It had devolved into a juvenile game and Finch knew it.

Tucker tilted his face toward the sky and screamed into the vast black above. "I just want an out!" He was tired. Tired of slinging crank. Tired of worrying day in and day out. Tired of being stuck under the thumb of not just Rawlins, but Darlene as well. Tired of her refusal to stop whoring herself out because, despite all the reasons she gave, she liked doing it, and for Tucker, that was the worst of it all. His love and her child weren't enough for her and never would be. He'd come to the realization a long time ago, but it was only now that he truly dwelled on it, that the only reason he stayed with her was that she was one of the few people who paid him any attention. Some people go their whole lives largely unnoticed by the rest of the population around them. Without Darlene, Tucker felt he'd be just another lonely soul walking the earth. But what was worse—living a life of loneliness or sharing the life you have with someone while begging them to see you? It was a hard pill to swallow, but it was the truth. They were just another statistic and Tucker wanted to be more than that.

Mavis watched from the sidelines as Tucker began to pace and relay his story to Finch. He told him how he came to be standing in the parking lot of The Blue Sparrow Inn, gun in hand, and his nerves about ready to split him in half. He spared no detail. He told him of his parents and upbringing, of resorting to crime and cooking crank. He told him of Darlene and the baby he loved who wasn't his. He told Finch about Rawlins and taking a cut from the drugs he sold and the dumping of BoDeen's body in Catalonia Lake. He hadn't intended to spill it all, but once he got going it was as if a pregnant woman somewhere inside him had just broken water and pushed it all out into the world, a messy delivery giving birth to all the awful things.

It was a lot to take in, but Finch stood in the cold of the night, in the parking lot of a bum fuck nowhere motel, and listened to the kid spill his guts, and it was clear that's all Tucker wanted. He just wanted someone to listen and validate the way he was feeling. When it was all over, the two men were leaning against the hood of the 64 Impala shooting the shit like they'd been childhood friends who hadn't seen each other in years and were just now catching up.

Finch fell into the conversation with ease. It had been a long time since he had someone to talk to. Someone he could even relate to. It reminded him of Colm and how much he missed having a brother. Someone who would listen without judgment, a person who would go to the grave with all your secrets no matter the cost.

"So let me get this straight, there's eighty-thousand dollars of drug money buried up on Durham Road?" Tucker pushed himself from the hood of the Impala, gun still planted firmly in his hand. His fingers were beginning to ache from holding it so tight.

"That's what I've been told, yes."

"And you want me to help you find it?"

"Four eyes are better than two."

"And you'll give me a cut?"

"A cut of the money for the gun, yes."

"Why?"

"Why what?"

"Why bring me in on this?"

Finch watched Tucker pace. He looked to Mavis who stood leaning against the façade of the motel next to the door of Finch's room, her hands tucked in her armpits.

"Do I have a choice," Finch said. "I need that gun and the only thing I have to offer as a trade is a cut of that money. I can also appreciate the sensitivity of your situation. Rawlins is doing to you what he's done to me and God knows how many others. He's got us both in a corner. You talk about wanting an out, well, I'm offering you a better deal than he is. I know what a pile of money can do for a poor man. Take a cut, leave, and never look back."

"So which one is it," Tucker asked.

"Take your pick, man. Whichever suites the narrative best and gets us what we both want."

"And what about her?" Tucker pointed to Mavis.

"What about her?"

"Is she in on this?"

"At this point, she could be. She's heard enough that she could easily ask for a cut. I'm not a greedy man and I'm certainly not my brother," Finch said.

"Meaning?" Tucker asked.

"Meaning that I'm not about to start offing people for a supposed cache of buried drug money." Finch looked at Mavis, the expression on his face clearly saying that he wanted to know where she stood on the situation.

"I don't even have an opinion. This is between y'all." She threw up her hands. "And as intrigued as I am, I've heard more than I wanted to, but to be honest, this Rawlins fella sounds like a real piece of work and he has whatever he's got coming to him," she said.

"You heard the lady," Finch said to Tucker. "Make your choice."

"And if I don't agree?"

"We go back out into the parking lot and resume our standoff."

"Not much of a standoff if I'm the only one with a gun," Tucker pointed out.

Finch shrugged his shoulders.

"You'll have to excuse my lack of enthusiasm," Tucker said. He'd stopped pacing and stood facing Finch. "It all just seems too convenient."

"Sometimes life has a way of sorting itself out," Finch said. "Not often, but sometimes. This seems to be one of those rare occasions."

Tucker extended his hand toward Finch. "Deal," Tucker said. Finch took Tucker's hand and they shook on it. "But I'm keeping the fuckin' gun until this is all over with."

17.

Abraham had taken the glass from the bathroom sink, the one motel staff put out for rinsing your mouth, and jammed the open end against the door of the motel room. He pushed his ear flat against its bottom and listened to the two men outside talk of buried drug money. Moments earlier he had witnessed their showdown through a slit in the curtains. One had nearly gotten shot, but not too soon after the confrontation had started, it devolved into one man pacing the gravel and nearly breaking down into tears as he told the other man a story that seemed fitting for a movie of the week.

He leaned away from the door, looked at the clock that sat on the bedside table, and wondered where Clem was. It had been a while since he'd left and there was still no sign of him. It never took this long to pull off a job. There was a feeling of something heavy moving through his guts like stones in a dryer. He went back to listening, pushing his ear back against the bottom of the glass, but little could be heard. Their voices had faded to near whispers. He approached the window and looked out. The two men were still there mewling around the Impala, its bottom going to rust, but the conversation seemed to be losing steam.

He tossed the glass on the bed where it landed next to the duffel bag, his gun still laid out on top of it. He paced the floor, his fingers locked behind his head. He began jumping up and down to keep his blood from going stagnant and cold with worry–anything to try and rid himself of the feeling that would soon turn frantic.

Then he heard it. Clem's voice. He couldn't hear the words being spoken, but Abraham knew it was his voice, the garbled words riding a violent and angry bark. It was a tone Abraham hadn't heard since they'd been in prison and because of this, he knew something was wrong.

Abraham rushed to the door, grabbing the 9mm from where it sat on his way past. He flung the door open and went headfirst into whatever waited on the other side.

/ / /

Clem moved like the wounded animal he was through the parking lot of the filling station and across the street toward The Blue Sparrow Inn, despite the heated pain radiating from his side and the wetness that had his shirt clinging to him like a sheet soaked in molasses. When he got closer to the parking lot of the motel, he heard voices, none of which he recognized, and as he advanced on those voices, he saw three figures crowding the area near the door to his room. With no resistance on his part, he dragged himself right into the middle of the action, needing only to get back to Abraham and lie down.

The three figures all looked in his direction at the same time, as if rehearsed. Confusion lit their faces. They stared at Clem, who looked like a pale imitation of a man. A ghost with a knife stuck in his ribs and a metal box stuffed under his arm, shotgun resting on his shoulder.

Tucker, who was fixated on the shotgun more than the man carrying it, swung his arm up and pointed the .38, a reaction that didn't register in his brain until he was aimed and steady, a finger already on the trigger.

Clem threw the shotgun forward with a jerk of his shoulder, the weight of the barrel almost too heavy for him to hold with one hand. Pain erupted from his ribcage, but he didn't let it show. He tightened the muscles in his face. Sweat beaded on his forehead. He kept the muzzle pointed between the two men and focused the mouth of the gun on the woman, who stood further back, against the façade of the building.

"I'd aim that gun elsewhere, hoss. This shotgun has a nice spread and all three of you are lined up perfectly in its sight," Clem said, nearly choking on his own pain.

Tucker knew the man wasn't bluffing because Tucker knew guns from years of hunting his own food. He also knew that the gun should always be a last resort and in that thought, he understood his father's actions as well as his own.

"We don't want any trouble, mister," Tucker said, gripping the handle of the revolver, tighter this time, in an attempt to keep himself from shaking and giving away the fact that he was nervous.

"That so? Is that why you're standing out here with a gun in your hand?" Clem asked. He looked at the three strangers whose expressions let him know that they didn't often have firearms pointed in their direction. He knew the look because he was a man who made it a habit of putting guns in people's faces.

"This ain't got nothin' to do with you," Finch said, pushing off from the front of the Impala and turning to face Clem.

"Ten minutes ago, I would have been inclined to agree," Clem said. "But seeing as it isn't ten minutes ago, seeing that it's right here, right now, I'd say it has a whole lot to do with me. And that gun your friend has pointed at my face proves I'm right." He spoke out of the side of his mouth and stood broad across the shoulders in a prison yard posture, two things he'd learned doing time in state penitentiaries all over the country. *"Always talk at an angle to keep lip readers in the dark and always stand like you're about ready to go to war,"* a cellmate had told him early on in his first stint.

Finch took notice.

"Just forget it happened. It was just a natural reaction," Tucker said.

"Ain't nothin' natural about pointing the busy end of a gun in someone's direction. Did anyone teach you manners or were all of you people here in Hicksville USA raised in a fucking barn?"

"I'll lower the gun, you can pass, and we can all be on our way." The words tumbled from Tucker's mouth in clips. He nearly choked trying to get them out.

"Too late for that. I don't take kindly to strangers pointing guns at me."

"I suppose we can say the same," Finch said.

"I suppose you can, but he drew first," Clem pointed out.

Finch let out a laugh.

"Is something funny?"

"I'm sorry, but what is this?"

"What is what?"

"This back and forth between us and you. I feel like we're in a western."

Hearing Finch's laugh cut loose a slab of anger in Clem that rode his blood like hot needles. He clenched his jaw and his lips curled, his face becoming flush, giving back some of the color he'd lost when he took a knife in the side. "It won't be funny when your head paints the windshield of that car," he said, the words aimed at Finch. He then looked to Tucker and said, "Drop the piece and kick it over to me or I will unload this gun into all three of you." His voice came out like a growl as if his throat was lined with sandpaper and it made Finch think of shit being scraped loose from a boot on brick. It echoed through the parking lot and escaped somewhere into the dark.

The banging of a door sounded from somewhere behind Tucker and Finch. A figure rushed past Mavis, but before she could warn anyone, Abraham was behind Finch, the 9mm jammed into the base of his skull.

"Do what he says, or I will fuckin' kill this man and bury him where he stands."

Tucker put up his hands, letting the .38 dangle from his index finger.

"That's right. Slowly," Abraham said.

Tucker, bending at the knees, lowered himself toward the ground and dropped the gun. He resumed a standing position and kicked the gun over to where Clem stood, whose face, once again was devoid of color, sweat like a waterfall leaking down his cheeks.

Abraham was looking at Clem from over Finch's shoulder. "You don't look so good, buddy."

"I don't doubt that. I don't feel so good," Clem said, letting out a slight laugh that was followed by a cough. He turned his torso to let Abraham get a glimpse of the knife. It was buried to the hilt. "Some bitch killed me."

"Fuck." Abraham's face went slack. He loosened his grip on the gun as he took in the sight of the man he loved looking like he was going to die right there but brushed away the feelings quickly and resumed his iron grip on the gun, applying pressure to the back of Finch's head before anyone got any bright ideas.

"We need to get them inside," Clem said. "I left a loose end and I suspect the place across the street is going to be crawling with cops soon." He squatted to retrieve the .38 that sat at his feet. He stayed hunched in that position for a few moments and drew a couple of deep breaths, bracing himself for the pain that standing up would ignite. Once he was stable, he and Abraham corralled the other three and marched them into the motel room from which Abraham had come.

18.

Clem was laid out on the bed feeling the full effect of his wound. The pain seemed to have tripled since he'd laid down, finally able to rest, leaving him with nothing to focus on except the fire and lightning that snaked its way out from the wound and through his body. The shotgun lay at his side, having traded it for the 9mm he'd tucked into his waistband earlier. He pointed the gun at the three figures that stood in the corner of the room while Abraham inspected the point of entry near Clem's ribcage.

"I can't get a good look at it with your jacket on and the damn thing is pinned to you. Can't take it off unless we pull out the knife and I'm not so sure that's a good idea. We might need to bite the bullet on this, Clem, and get you to a hospital."

"Not an option."

"I don't know what else to do, man. This is bad."

"There's nothing to look at, I know it's bad. I'm the one feeling it. I got stabbed and that's the end of it. I'm not walking around with this thing in me, so pull it out and do it now." Clem looked at Abraham whose eyes lingered on the knife handle. "Do it, or I will."

"If either of us removes that knife, you're going to die," said Abraham. "It's deep and there's no telling what kind of damage it's done internally."

"I'm alright with that."

"Maybe I'm not."

"You have to be."

"What if I can't?"

"Then you'll go back to prison and I'll die anyway."

"Why can't we just hit the hospital and deal with the repercussions later?"

"There won't be a later," Clem said, his voice rising. "I fuckin' killed the guy."

"Jesus Christ."

"It was an accident. His daughter was in there. Must have been in the back room. She came up behind me and hit me with a jab and my finger let off a round."

"And where is she now?"

"She's the loose end I was referring to."

"Fuck."

"Yeah, no shit. So we don't have a lot of time. Now get this out of me." Clem looked at Mavis and recognized her as the girl from the front desk when he and Abraham had checked in that morning, something he hadn't noticed when they were all standing in the dimly lit parking lot moments earlier. "You got a first aid kit of some kind in this place?"

"There's one in the office, but I'm not sure what's left in it," she answered. "Been picked clean over the years and you're gonna need more than band-aids and Neosporin for that boo-boo."

"Fuckin' comedian over there," Clem said. He looked to Abraham. "Take her to the office and get what you can."

"I can't leave you here with the other two," Abraham protested.

"I got this," Clem said, bringing his attention back to Tucker and Finch. He pointed at each of them with the muzzle of the gun and said, "My friend here is gonna take her to the office to get that kit. We're not gonna do anything stupid while they're gone, now are we? Because if there's a problem, my friend won't hesitate to off the broad."

Tucker and Finch agreed with a shake of their heads.

"Let's go," Abraham said to Mavis. She moved from the corner of the room and came to stand beside Abraham who turned her around toward the door and held the 9mm to her back. They proceeded to the doorway where Abraham said, "Clem, what's the plan after we get this knife out of you?" He didn't turn to speak, just spoke the words to the back of Mavis' head.

"Get on out of here and drive until I expire."

Abraham didn't have a response. It was something he didn't even want to think about, but he was suddenly being forced to envision the rest of his life without the man he loved knowing Clem was a dead man. All their plans were down the toilet because of some pipedream that Abraham could never truly live his life the way he felt he needed to, which didn't seem as important now if Clem couldn't survive to share it with him.

He nudged Mavis with the gun, she opened the door, and they were gone from the room.

/ / /

In the office, Mavis told Abraham that the first aid kit was in the back room, behind the desk. He waved the gun forward, signaling for her to keep moving, which she did. Once in the backroom, Abraham stood in the doorway and watched Mavis search for the white kit with the red cross on its lid.

She walked to a file cabinet first and checked on top, moving some papers and various items. There was a potted plant that sat dead center which she slid over a few inches to check behind it, finding nothing but magazines she'd read a hundred times that had been left to collect dust.

She turned and met Abraham's gaze for a second but quickly averted her eyes and focused on the task at hand. She rummaged through the drawers of a desk that was pushed up against the wall. Like the file cabinet, its top was littered with papers and receipts, along with a stack of black binders filled with pages that contained the names of every guest that had stayed in The Blue Sparrow Inn for the last six months.

"Your friend is going to die if you don't get him to a hospital. That wound looked pretty severe," she said, as she continued to dig through a drawer, not wanting to look at Abraham for fear of what she might see in his eyes.

"Lover."

"Excuse me?" She stopped her search, keeping her back to him and waited for a response.

"He's not my friend, he's my lover," Abraham said, correcting her as if Mavis calling Clem his friend had offended him. And, in a way, it did. Their relationship was so much deeper and was rooted in something far more profound than just a prison friendship.

"Oh. Well, all the more reason to get him to a hospital, I suppose."

"I wish that were an option, but Clem has already made up his mind and once that happens, there's no steering him in a different direction. Not even his own death would convince him otherwise." Abraham shifted in the doorway and cleared his throat. "And to be honest, he'll probably die even if I do get him to a hospital. He's lost a lot of blood already and the wound is pretty deep. God only knows how sanitary that knife was."

Mavis went back to searching for the first aid kit, finally finding it in the bottom drawer buried beneath a few decks of playing cards and a set of screwdrivers stored in a black pouch. "Here it is," she said, placing the box on the desk and opening its lid. "There isn't a whole lot in here. Some gauze, a few adhesive strips. A roll of bandages." She looked over her shoulder at Abraham.

"It'll have to do. Let's get back to the room."

Abraham shifted, making room for Mavis to join him in the doorway. She stood holding the kit in both hands, palms extended flat like it was some thousand-year-old religious relic that needed to be handled with care, and maybe it was just as important considering it could be her key to surviving this situation.

"You got a safe in here?" Abraham asked.

"Yeah, behind that picture," she motioned to a picture on the wall above the desk with a jerk of her head.

Abraham eyed the framed photo from the threshold. He saw Mavis in the photo crammed between three other figures that he assumed were her parents and, possibly, a brother. They all had their arms around each other and, aside from the younger male, they were all smiling. His face seemed indifferent to whatever was happening, a faraway look in his eyes that held a sadness that seemed to go on forever. Abraham knew that look. He'd lived for a long time with that same expression sculpted into his own face. It isn't hard when you spend most of your life feeling like a scream without a mouth to escape from. He reached up to touch his cheeks with his fingertips but was severed from the moment as Mavis' voice cut through the silence.

"You gonna take what's in there?"

"I was thinking about it, but we've already put you through enough tonight. No need to go adding insult to injury." He took one last glance at the giant black and white photograph and then said, "I'm gonna say this here because I won't say it in front of Clem, but for what it's worth, I'm sorry. This wasn't how it was supposed to go."

"I didn't know holding people at gunpoint was supposed to go a certain way." She looked into Abraham's eyes and saw remorse and wetness beginning to form around the edges, and she knew he was telling the truth. "But thank you."

He took Mavis by the shoulder and pointed her in the direction of the exit. On their way out from behind the desk, he spotted a bottle sitting on a stool, a worm suspended in its contents.

"What's this?" He asked and pointed to the bottle.

"Homemade mescal."

Abraham hooked his finger in the opening of the bottleneck and pushed her forward and out the door.

/ / /

Back in the room, Abraham and Mavis found Clem, Tucker, and Finch in the same spots they had left them. After a few moments of conversation that added up to nothing, Abraham gathered some towels from the bathroom, sat on the bed, and asked, "You ready?"

Clem said no but told him to do it anyway.

Abraham wound up a washcloth and stuffed it in Clem's mouth, telling him to bite down. Then he flanked the hilt of the knife between two fingers, applied pressure to the area surrounding the entry point, and waited for a three-count before he pulled the knife loose from Clem's side. Clem's muffled screams tore through the rag and filled the room. He sounded like a man losing a war he couldn't afford to as blood escaped and bubbled in leaky gulps. It was a scream that could have stopped traffic.

Finch watched from the corner of the room as it all played out, his mind going a mile a minute, hoping to come to some revelation that would help him and the other two find some balance in the situation. But there was nothing.

Abraham took the other towel from his lap with one hand and covered the wound to soak up some of the blood. With the other hand, he held up the bottle of mescal and undid the cap with his teeth. He spat the cap onto the bed, pushed away the flap of Clem's jacket to better expose the hole he had punched into his ribs, and doused it with a steady stream of mescal, making sure the worm did not escape. Instant heat erupted as if someone had started a fire from inside the incision. Clem writhed and screamed again. His legs jerked and flailed, his knees coming up and nearly making contact with Abraham's face.

"Stay still, fucker," Abraham said, but Clem didn't hear him as he bucked and jerked, the pain having him praying for death. He'd been cut before, many times in prison altercations, but nothing compared to this.

"What's in the bottle?" Clem asked Abraham.

"Toilet made mescal."

"Give it to me." Clem held out his hand and Abraham passed him the bottle. He watched as Clem nearly emptied the rest down his throat. It went down as smooth as gasoline and Clem choked on the burn.

After removing Clem's jacket and shirt, Abraham dressed the wound in gauze and wrapped his midsection in bandages. He dabbed the sweat from Clem's forehead.

"That's as good as I'm going to be able to do, but I'm still of the opinion that we should consider getting your ass to a person with a clue." Abraham leaned into Clem and their lips met. Tucker and Finch averted their gaze as if they were bearing witness to a moment too intimate for an audience. Mavis watched, almost wishing the two of them the best, so long as Finch, Tucker, and herself didn't have to pay a price for it to happen. Despite the situation that she found herself in, Abraham and Clem seemed to have a genuine love for each other, and she found it touching, even felt herself rooting for them.

Abraham had taken note of their wandering eyes and felt a push of uncomfortable air between him and them. He stood up and asked, "Do prison fags make you uncomfortable, or is it that I'm black and gay?"

"Maybe it's that's we're interracially homosexual," Clem said, sitting up and wincing through his teeth. You know how these rural bumpkins roll."

"Is that it? You peckerwoods don't like interracial homos?"

"What I think is beside the point," Tucker said.

"What about you?" Abraham looked to Finch.

"The only problem I have is that I'm being held against my will over something I really don't give a shit about," he said. "I have my own concerns and I don't need to be hauling yours around too."

"Oh, that's right." Abraham rounded the corner of the bed, sweeping up the 9mm from the tussled blankets as he did, and stood facing the three figures in the corner of the room. He pointed the gun at Tucker and Finch. "You two have a big expedition ahead of you."

"What's going on?" Clem asked. He swung his legs over the edge of the bed and braced himself to lift off the mattress. He stood, some of the pain having lost its edge due to the mescal he'd consumed. And the fact he no longer had a knife digging at his insides.

"In all this excitement I almost forgot to tell you." Abraham smiled.

"Tell me what?" Clem's face went to stone.

"Before you showed up, these two were about ready to off each other. That is until this handsome fucker..." Abraham gripped Finch by the shoulder and for the first time, Finch got a better understanding of the sheer muscle this man was the owner of. He didn't just look the part; he was a fucking machine. Veins like tightropes lined his arm as he gripped Finch's shoulder more tightly. The kind of veins a junkie would be jealous of. Finch thought the pain would bring him to his knees. "...cut a deal with that scraggly fucker there." Abraham put the barrel of the 9mm in Tucker's face. "Eighty grand of buried drug money somewhere up in these hills."

"Is that so?"

"I heard it all from in here. Was listening through the door the whole time they were out there."

"What about her?" Clem pointed a finger at Mavis.

"I'm not sure how she fits in. She was quiet the whole time these two were bickering like an old couple. Honestly didn't even know she was there until I came out for you."

"Looks like our plans have changed." Clem looked at Finch. "You're gonna take us to this money and this time, no deals."

Finch thought of Maggie and Sarah. Thought of Colm and his last dying wish being hijacked by a pair of criminals no different than himself in some ways. He felt a rush of rage galloping through him like a herd of bulls. He tightened his hands into fists, wanting to let loose into Clem's face.

"Over my dead fuckin' body," Finch said, with nothing to back up the comment.

"Yeah? Well, what about hers instead?" Clem stepped toward Mavis and without further warning, raised the 9mm he'd been holding and shot her in the mouth.

For a few hot white seconds, Tucker and Finch watched as Mavis' body was lifted up by the force of the shot and slammed onto her back, eyes filled with blinding fire from the muzzle. She was staring upward as if the answer to a question she'd been asking her entire life was written across the ceiling. But she wasn't dead, nor had she even begun to die. Stunned, wounded, and bleeding from the face, she lay in pain and shock, and as Clem approached her, she didn't seem to notice him. Her eyes stayed glued to the ceiling above. He lifted the gun once more and fired two more rounds into her chest.

Clem's face held no emotion, but his eyes bore a thousand-yard stare, reducing his features to a blank slate, which had been bred into him from all the years of witnessing or participating in prison yard brawls that left their mark on his psyche. He had let one woman live only to take the life of another.

Life, if nothing else, is all about balance, Clem thought.

/ / /

Seeing something like that changes everything. For a few brief moments that seemed to last forever, nothing else drew breath, least of all the woman lying on the floor. It was just Tucker and Finch existing in a tiny bubble with only what had just happened staring them in the face. Tunnel vision followed. No noise. No feeling they would ever be able to explain. Just their guts being turned upside down.

And then suddenly there were voices coming from somewhere inside the room. They came on in bursts of clipped and frenzied speech, but neither Finch nor Tucker could hear the words because they were buried beneath the sound of gunfire still ringing in their ears.

For the two of them, the room seemed to bob and weave like a ship caught in bad weather as figures rushed past them, left then right and back again, while Clem and Abraham gathered up anything they might need. Tucker couldn't be sure, but he thought he may have leaned forward to puke onto the carpet, a lingering taste in his mouth confirming his suspicion. Finch held his arm out and felt for the wall behind him to keep himself from going down. And then, just as quickly as all their senses returned, they were being pushed from the room, guns pressed into the smalls of their backs, and forced into the gravel grey Plymouth.

Finch was at the wheel. Tucker sat shotgun. Abraham and Clem were in the back seat with the guns resting on the seat in front of them, aimed and ready to do to Finch and Tucker what Clem had done to Mavis if they didn't comply. For Finch, the voice was still far away, as if it were traveling from some hidden room at the end of a long and empty hallway. He felt the cold steel of a gun jab him in the back of his skull and he knew it was the snub-nosed revolver. He'd pressed the muzzle of that gun to his own head a thousand times, threatening his brother's taunts. There was a familiar feeling of comfort that came along with the way the mouth of the revolver fit snugly in that dip at the base of his skull and suddenly the voice talking came to him clear as crystal.

It told him to drive.

19.

Sheriff Lou Rawlins got the call at a quarter after two in the morning informing him of a robbery that left one dead and another with a serious case of trauma from which she may never recover. After securing his mother to her bed with medical straps and calling Lucinda asking if she could come to watch Lynette, he dressed, got in the cruiser, and left.

By the time he arrived at the two-pump filling station on the stretch of road connecting Fulton to Greensborough, a whole slew of cops already had the place taped off. Clusters of red and blue lights swirled, illuminating the surrounding area that was otherwise dark. Rawlins stepped from the cruiser and limped over to Deputy Eugene Plank who stood talking to a woman. She sat in the back seat of a patrol car with the door open, her feet on the ground, wrapped in a blanket. Her hands pinched it together and kept it tucked under her chin.

"Fuck of a mess, Sheriff," Eugene said as Rawlins approached.

Rawlins led Deputy Plank out of the woman's earshot and said, "I gathered that much from the phone call. Has she said anything yet?"

"She called in, absolutely hysterical, saying that her father had been shot during a robbery." He looked down at a notepad he held in his hand and flipped a page. "She was in the back room while most of the robbery went down. The guy must not have known she was in there helping him close shop. She came out of the backroom and stuck the perp with a knife."

"She stabbed the guy?"

"Yeah, said she got him pretty good too. We should alert the nearby hospitals to keep an eye out. Anyway, that's when he fired and cut down Old Man Hoffstetter. Then he forced her out back to the church, took the donation box, and left. Told her to pray."

"Jesus Christ."

"Yeah, the whole thing seems strange."

"Fuckin' shame. I've known Jacob Hoffstetter my whole life."

"A lot of us have, Sir."

Rawlins stood with his hands on his hips. He looked back to the woman, still wrapped tightly in the blanket, a look of pure devastation cut deep into her face. "Did she give a description?" Rawlins asked without turning his head, his eyes cemented on the woman who was now the poster child for loss in Rawlins' mind.

"Took her a minute to get it out, but she did." Deputy Plank flipped back a couple of pages in his notepad. "White. Late thirties, early forties. Average height with a semi muscular build. She said it was hard to tell though because he wore a black trench coat. He was also wearing blue pants, the kind mechanics wear. Dirty blonde hair that was shaved on the sides with a bit more left on top, and he had on thick-framed glasses." Plank looked to Rawlins who was still staring in the woman's direction. He seemed to look through her, his gaze was so fixated. "Oh, and he had a mustache as well." Rawlins didn't respond. "What are you thinking, Sir?"

"I'm thinking I need a cigarette and a vacation, Eugene."

"Weird thing about the description, it doesn't fit Tucker Fodee or BoDeen Carlson."

Rawlins finally dragged his vision away from the direction of the woman and cold stared at Deputy Plank. "Come again?"

"Well, neither Tucker nor BoDeen fit the description, but that is Tucker's truck over there, is it not?" Plank pointed past Rawlins, past the cluster of cop cars and yellow tape, and to the edge of the parking lot where the siren lights didn't quite reach.

Rawlins saw the Bronco parked quietly at the edge of the lot and wondered how he'd missed it when he first arrived. Then he wondered where the hell Tucker was and thought about the cluster fuck this was turning into.

"You might want to call your sister, Sir."

"Yeah," Rawlins said, practically shrugging off Plank's comment. He turned and faced The Blue Sparrow Inn across the street and saw the Impala still parked. Then he noticed light spilling from an open motel room door. *Where the fuck are you, Tucker,* he thought.

/ / /

Rawlins left Deputy Eugene Plank in charge at the gas station, warning him not to talk to any reporters should they happen to show up. It wasn't likely, given that Fulton barely had a newspaper or local news channel, and neither were staffed with people eager to get the jump on a story this time of night, but he felt the need to say it to Plank regardless. The guy was a "dimwit", as his father would have put it.

He lit a cigarette and crossed the street, explaining that he was going to ask the woman who ran the motel if she had seen anything suspicious or had any off-colored guests, but his real reason was to check up on that open door. He'd watched it like a hawk for a few minutes while Plank prattled on, his voice distant in Rawlins' head. At first, Rawlins thought that maybe the room's occupant had left it open purposefully for whatever reason, but as time crawled with no sign of life and no movement, the nagging feeling that something else was going on crept up the back of his neck. Exactly what, he couldn't say, but with Tucker's Bronco parked at the scene of a murder, Tucker missing, and Finch's Impala still parked in the motel lot, it wasn't adding up to anything good.

Halfway through the parking lot, he threw his cigarette into a puddle, the reflection of the motel's neon sign breaking in the ripples before coming back into focus. He approached the Impala, peeked into its window, and saw nothing put papers and napkins strewn along the seats.

Outside the motel door, Rawlins unholstered his gun and called out to anyone who might be in the room. "This is Sheriff Lou Rawlins with the Fulton Police Department. If anyone is in there, please identify yourself."

There was no response.

Rawlins held his gun up with one hand, gripped the bottom of his palm with the other, and rounded the door jamb, anticipating what might be lying in wait. He was met with an empty room. The blankets on the bed were tousled and tossed, a bloody t-shirt lying on top of them. He eyed the bathroom door that sat just beyond the bed, cleared his throat, and called out again, this time his voice a bit more earth-shattering. "If anyone is here, come out with your hands up!"

Again, nothing.

His eyes moved from the bathroom door to the mess of sheets and then to the floor. That's when he saw a pair of feet peeking out from behind the bed. He approached slowly until the body revealed itself. It looked like she'd been thrown to the floor, her upper half lying in the bathroom, while her lower half came to rest across the threshold. Blood pooled around her head, making a mess across the tiles. Two more bullet wounds in her chest.

"What the fuck," Rawlins whispered to himself before thinking, *Forget about any two-bit reporter from Fulton, every fuckin' hack from Greensborough is gonna be all over this shit storm.*

20.

Finch white-knuckled the steering wheel of the Plymouth, the gun pressed to the back of his skull louder than anything he'd experienced in his entire life. Tucker had his hands extended, gripping the dashboard, the image of the muzzle flash and the woman's eyes stitched to her forehead still flickering in his mind. He'd been in the drug business for a few years now, but he wasn't like these guys in the back seat, and it was guys like them he'd be sleeping, eating, and shitting next to if his plan didn't pan out, and at that moment, there wasn't much in Tucker's favor.

He wasn't a hardened criminal. He was a kid who sought the only opportunities that he could get. For the first time since he'd watched his father kill his mother, Tucker was scared for his life. It seemed to fringe his entire being. The hair on the back of his neck stood up and his guts were doing loops over themselves, tangles forming. He wanted to puke again, but there was nothing left in his stomach. He side-eyed Finch to see if he looked as nervous as he himself felt, but nothing was evident.

Finch gunned the car down the strip of uneven road, the black of night hurling itself at the windshield, and the headlights carving out a tunnel of light for which to pass through.

"You might want to slow down there, boss," Clem said from the back seat.

"Do you wanna drive instead?"

"I'm telling you to slow down." Clem pushed the gun harder into the back of Finch's head.

"Or what? You'll shoot me and kill yourself and your boyfriend in the process. Go ahead."

Clem opened his mouth, but Abraham spoke before Clem could get the words out, aiming to deflect an already bad situation from getting worse.

"How far is this place?" Abraham asked.

"The road is only a couple more miles, but as far as the trailer where the money is supposedly buried, I have no idea. Could be a few feet off the main road or miles past where the road ends." Finch clenched his teeth, fighting the urge to sabotage the whole thing and flip the car on purpose, ending it all right there. He looked at the speedometer. The needle teetered between fifty-five and sixty. A little more speed and he'd have enough momentum to straddle the shoulder of the road and flip the car on its head with a jerk of the wheel.

Clem's voice came again from behind Finch like a bad penny. "I said to slow the fuck down, you're gonna lose it and kill us all."

Finch eyed Clem's reflection in the rearview mirror. "Now you're gettin' the idea."

Clem looked at Abraham and said, "If this son of a bitch doesn't slow down by the count of five, I want you to put a bullet through his buddy's head."

"There's no reason for all of this, guys." Abraham turned to look at Clem. "If what he says is true, there's plenty for all of us."

"I said no deals. I'm done playing nice."

"Done?" Finch laughed. "For you to be done, you'd have to have been playing nice in the first place. Your introduction was sticking a shotgun in our faces and then killing a woman who had nothing to do with any of this." His eyes moved from the road to the rearview mirror and back again.

"On the count of five," Clem repeated to Abraham.

Tucker gripped the dashboard tighter. He thought his fingernails were going to break. He shut his eyes and waited for the blast.

"I'm not doing this." Abraham lowered his gun. Tucker opened his eyes, unable to stop the small sigh of relief escaping his chest.

"Excuse me?"

"You heard me."

"This is not the fucking time."

"It is absolutely the time."

"I'm doing this for you."

"You keep saying that, but I'm starting to think this has become something else entirely. The woman back at the motel, she didn't deserve that. Likewise for the old man at the gas station."

"I told you the old man was an accident."

"And that somehow makes it better? This has gone further than I wanted it to. We don't have to do it like this."

"Yes, we do."

"Why?" Abraham's eyes pleaded with Clem to see reason.

There was a moment of silence you could cut with a knife.

Clem's eyelids went heavy, nearly closing and shutting out the visual of Abraham next to him. The expression on Abraham's face was like that of a child's, wondering why he was being punished. The whole scene stuck Clem in the chest and he felt a flutter in his guts like a bird flapping its wings to rid itself of rainwater.

"Because I'm fading here, brother. This is the last chance that I've got to make things right. Everything I've done. Now, you take that gun and on the count of five, do what I asked."

Abraham released his grip on the pistol and let it fall to the space between them. Even in the dark interior of the back seat, he could see the muscles along Clem's jawline tighten as he let out a sigh of frustration.

"Fine," Clem said, "I'll do it." He swung his gun away from Finch's head and stuck it into Tucker's temple, forcing his head to the right. Tucker felt his neck crack.

With his head cocked sideways, Tucker continued to grip the dash with one hand while the other went down his shirt to retrieve his father's AA chip that hung from a pull chain. He pulled it free and pressed it to his lips, not knowing what good it was going to do or if the gesture was worth anything, but when a gun is pressed to a man's head, he'll do anything to try to make himself feel better. Or at least to take his mind off the fact.

Either way, it didn't work.

Finch eyed Tucker from the corner of his eye and wondered what the hell he was doing. More than anything, he saw a kid brimming with fear and probably wondering how the hell he ended up in the front seat of a beat-up Plymouth captained by a trained thief and two ex-cons in the backseat, one of whom was ready to turn his head to pudding.

Shit, Finch wondered the same for himself.

Finch heard the click-back of the hammer and thought, *I can't let this kid's death be on my conscience. It's already crowded in there with too many voices as it is, and it gets awfully loud and confusing when I'm drunk and everyone is talking at once. Plus, Colm will be joining the rest of the choir soon enough.*

From the front seat, Finch said, "Okay, fuck. I'll slow down. Just unbury the gun from the kid's head."

Clem waited to feel the car's momentum slow and then he released the gun from Tucker's head and brought it back to Finch's.

"Any more stunts like that and I will not give warning," Clem said and eased himself back against the seat.

/ / /

Finch steered the Plymouth up a mud-covered road that eventually dead-ended when the woods became too thick, the overgrowth having swallowed the rest of the old switchback. The car came to a stop and Finch put it in park and turned off the ignition.

"This is as far as we can go in this thing."

"Now what?" Tucker asked. He looked in Finch's direction, but Finch stared ahead through the windshield. Tucker worked his hand over his neck, massaging out a kink.

Clem shifted, keeping the gun on Finch, and reached into the pocket of his jacket to retrieve a pack of cigarettes. He lit one and said, "Now we wait for first light, and we go find ourselves a treasure." He took long slow drags of the cigarette. The car filled with smoke and hung like fog across a barren field.

"Are you sure you're up for this?" Abraham asked.

"I don't have a choice now. Not after the fuckery that occurred tonight. I didn't come this far to just throw up my hands." He blew smoke from his nose, handed the cigarette to Abraham, and the two of them continued the process until there was nothing left but the filter. Clem dropped the butt to the floorboard and stomped it out with his boot. His head began to waver, suddenly feeling like a bowling ball about ready to roll off his shoulders. He didn't look good. Worse than before. He was pale again and sweating. All the excitement the car ride had offered had sapped him of any energy he had left. Abraham would be surprised if he made it a couple more hours.

"You keep an eye on these two. I just need to rest my head for a bit." Clem picked up the gun from the spot Abraham had dropped it and held it out for him to take, which he did. Then he rested his head against Abraham's shoulder. He coughed and tasted blood but choked it back and kept this new development to himself. "Don't you two go trying to pull a Houdini," Clem said before shifting his eyes up toward Abraham, "These two try anything, you know what to do."

Abraham rested his head against Clem's, keeping the gun low but ready.

"Hey," Clem whispered.

"Yeah?"

"Brooklynn."

"What?"

"Brooklynn. With two n's. It's a good name for when the time comes."

Abraham kissed Clem on top of his head and said, "I think I like it." But Clem didn't hear him because he was already sleeping and on his way to dying. He snored slightly through shallow breathing and Abraham hoped that Clem was having one last good dream.

21.

What felt like only minutes turned out to be nearly an hour. Abraham stared out the window as the other three snored. Aside from Clem, Abraham couldn't understand how anyone found sleep. The sky was lined with thinning clouds. Light escaped through a hole and caused a shaft of light. It was a visual Abraham's mother always referred to as 'Bible Sky.'

He woke the others and told them it was time, different motives fueling each of them as they stepped from the car and into the gray wash of morning.

Abraham stretched and asked, "Which direction do we go?" He walked to the back of the car and opened the trunk to retrieve a duffel bag. He unzipped it and dumped its contents, then slung the weightless sack over his shoulder.

Finch watched and said, "As far as I know we keep heading up this road. The trailer is located somewhere on either side. We should be able to spot it though, through the thinning trees."

Clem held himself up by leaning against the car, but he wanted to lie down and die. Instead, he reached for his side, felt a tug of pain, and then realized he'd been bleeding. It had soaked through the bandages and ran in rivulets to the waist of his pants, some areas having already dried. He did his best to ignore it, as did Abraham, knowing that bringing it up would only cause anger on Clem's part.

"You two are leading the way." Clem motioned for Finch and Tucker to start walking and they weaved themselves through years of nearly impenetrable pine saplings, coming out on the other side where the road continued up at an
incline and bent away and out of sight.

Abraham and Clem followed.

/ / /

An hour passed and the four of them had cleared two miles through the woods without saying much to each other, all four keeping their eyes peeled for anything that resembled the remains of a trailer. What was once a service road laid with gravel was now whittled down to a trail, years of snow and heavy rain washing most of it away. The wind shifted and carried with it the awful smell of decay and rot.

Abraham put his arm up to cover his nose and said, "What the hell is that smell?"

"Smells like something's dead." Clem laughed through a cough.

"Must be close to Myer Ridge," Tucker said. "It's the place they dump all the roadkill. You should smell it in the summer." Even though it was a chilly autumn morning, Tucker had begun to sweat from hiking the two miles. He removed his mesh cap, dabbed at his forehead with the sleeve of his jacket, and then replaced the cap on his head.

"I'm good on that," Abraham said. "Smells worse than the prison toilets I had to clean when I was on the inside. Didn't think it got much worse than prison food being emptied through the bowels of men who took it up the ass."

"Lovely image," Finch said.

"Should have been there."

Tucker stopped and stared through a crop of trees. "I think I found it," he said.

The others halted and followed his gaze. On the other side of a cluster of trees and ground covered thick with deadfall was a clearing. At its center, the husk of a trailer, its siding having gone black from fire.

/ / /

The trailer stood on cinder blocks, giving a person just enough room between its bottom and the ground to crawl underneath.

Looks like there may be some validity to Colm's claim of buried money, Finch thought.

"What happens if the money is here," Finch asked, turning away from the trailer to face Clem who stood leaning to one side. He was shirtless, but still wore his jacket and Finch eyed the tattoo across his chest. He kept the gun low, his finger on the trigger but not aimed at anyone or anything in particular.

"We call it a day. Then Abraham and I take it and drive on out of here."

"I mean, what happens to us?" Finch motioned to Tucker and himself with his index finger.

"I don't care what happens to you two, but I'm not going to kill you if that's what you're asking. Assuming you don't give us any more trouble and you hand over the findings without a fight." Clem stepped toward Tucker and cracked him over the top of his head with the butt of the revolver. Tucker went to his knees, feeling as if something had been torn loose inside his skull. Clem yanked him back to his feet, pressed the gun to his neck, and said, "But we ain't found the money yet, so get under there and start diggin'. I'm ready to be done with this."

Finch dropped to his stomach and, for a few brief moments, thought of Colm assuming the same position, alone in his cell, seven days a week, to do two-hundred pushups at a clip, bulking up and readying himself for his final walk and his final show of defiance. He shook the thought loose from his head, pushed off from the ground with the tips of his toes, and slid himself into the damp shade under the trailer. He scanned the area, looking for any indication of where something might be buried, an indentation, or a place where the ground looked to be cut away, but it was wishful thinking because he saw nothing as his eyes adjusted to the dimness.

"Might be a good idea for you to go round back of this shit box in case he crawls out on the other side and tries to make a run for it," Clem said to Abraham.

Finch watched Abraham's lower half move away from the other two and take a position on the other side of the trailer. Then he picked a spot and started clawing at the dirt. The smell of wet soil and mildew filled his nose. Insects revealed themselves as he moved earth away from earth. The trailer wasn't big by any means, but it was big enough for Finch to not get far digging at the area it covered alone. It would take all day and into the night. He could do it, but there was no telling where it was or how far down it was buried.

"This would be a lot easier if two people were under here looking," Finch called out.

"You can just forget it," Clem said.

"You'll be dead before I find it. There's too much ground to cover and it's not like I have a map with a giant X on it."

Abraham spoke up. "He may have a point, Clem. We need to hightail it as soon as possible. Someone is gonna discover the bodies you left behind, if they haven't already, and then it'll be cops from one end of the road to the other. If we're gonna do this, we need to do it and get a move on."

"Fine, fuck me then. What do I know? Abraham, if you wanna get under there and start diggin' then by all means…"

Abraham dropped the duffel he still had slung over his shoulder, got low to the ground, and belly crawled under the trailer to join Finch. He began digging with one hand while the other kept a grip on his 9mm.

"Might be easier if you lose the gun."

"Not gonna happen."

"Can't blame a man for trying."

Finch and Abraham kept at it, sweating as they dug into the ground with their bare hands, some areas proving more difficult than others to loosen the soil without the proper tools. Finch still didn't have a plan. He thought of Maggie and Sarah, thought of them losing the house on account of two ex-convicts, and he wanted to sink into the earth and stay there. It was his last shot at delivering something that could save them, but there was no way out of this. What he'd done to others for years was now coming back to take a chunk out of his ass, but it wasn't Finch that would have to suffer the consequences.

Finch's fingers felt arthritic by the time he came across a piece of wood covered with a thin layer of dirt. He brushed the soil and mud away to reveal a 6x6 piece of plywood that acted as a cover to a hole that held a box.

"I think I got something," Finch said as he pulled the box loose from the ground.

Abraham slid himself along the mud-caked ground to where Finch was sprawled out. The box rested between them. In the cramped space, they could feel each other's breath on their faces. They were both winded and their chests heaved as they both took in lungfuls of air, the damp smell of earth and rainwater not helping them in their attempts. Both men coughed.

"I'll let you do the honors," Abraham said.

"Why? It's not like I'll get to keep it."

"Just open it." Abraham held the gun on Finch.

Finch peeled back the four flaps of the box. Inside were stacks of rubber-banded bills, the weather having taken a toll on them. There was no way to tell how much was there without counting, but it was something even if it wasn't as much as there was rumored to be.

"We got it," Abraham called out. But there was no reply. Just the sound of a body thudding along the ground, followed by a visual of feet scrambling across fallen leaves.

22.

The clouds had finally broken up, letting the sun through. Several days of rain and it was finally going to be a beautiful day with a blue sky that went on forever. Clem had his head tilted back and was letting the sun warm his face. Cold chills were running up and down his spine again. He lit a cigarette and took long slow drags, coughing as he did. His lungs felt like they were stuffed with static and smoking only made it worse, but he refused to put it out, knowing what his fate was. He was close and he knew it, but damn if that sun didn't make him feel alive. It was one of the things he'd missed most when he was on the inside, especially in the summer. Barbecues with friends and trips to the beach with lovers. It was his favorite time of year. Sometimes he'd lay on his bunk after lights out and call up the sound of the ocean, its pounding roar and rush of water pumping through his eardrums. It lulled him to sleep most nights, and on the nights it didn't, he just imagined he was there after nightfall watching the waves roll in and lap at the edges of the sand, only to call itself back out again, over and over. It was easy to lose himself in that scenario and he did as he held the snub-nosed revolver to the back of some kid's head. Some kid he didn't know. He almost felt bad, but he also felt justified in that he never got a fair shake so why give someone else a chance?

"You believe in God, kid?" Clem tossed the butt of his cigarette to the ground and looked ahead, the waves and salty breeze receding further into the back of his mind.

"Not particularly. I used to when I was a kid. Back before life happened."

"That's too bad."

"And why is that?"

"If you did, you could start praying your buddy finds this money."

"He's not my buddy."

"Well, whatever the fuck he is to you."

"I thought you said you weren't going to kill us." Tucker felt his heart crawl an inch toward his throat. He swallowed hard.

"I said I wasn't going to kill you if he found the money. No money, no deal."

"What's the difference if he finds it or not?"

"The difference will be my mood."

"So, I'll die based on something that's out of anyone's control? You seem to have some anger issues that need addressing."

"Of course I'm angry, who isn't? You're not?"

"I would never deny that I am. There's a lot to be angry about. I'm just not gonna shoot people over it. It has nothing to do with them."

"Who's them?"

"The general 'them'."

"Well isn't that noble of you," Clem said.

They both went quiet for a few moments. Clem stood hunched at an angle, fighting the urge to drop into the dirt. Blood continued to push its way from his wound, the gauze and bandages becoming soaked like a well-worn dishrag. He closed his eyes, feeling his head go lightweight. He drew deep breaths and then threw his shoulders back, forcing himself to stand at attention. He opened his eyes and said, "Shit, I'm not even sure what we're talking about at this point, but what I do know is that life ain't nothin' but a loan shark exacting a very high-interest rate for the few pleasures it offers. I don't have time to play by the rules. I take whatever it is I need when the opportunities present themselves, and by any means necessary."

Tucker didn't say anything simply because there was nothing to say. He certainly understood where Clem was coming from, Tucker just wished he didn't have to pay the price for this man's beliefs.

"Fuck," Clem mumbled.

"You alright back there?"

Clem laughed. "Not so much, kid." He stumbled back trying to catch himself but failing in the attempt and as he did, Tucker felt the pressure of the muzzle at the back of his head lift, followed by the *thud* of Clem hitting the ground, and just like Clem had said about taking opportunities when they present themselves, so did Tucker.

He scrambled for a moment, turned to face Clem, and without thinking about it, kicked Clem in the face, crushing his nose and busting his glasses with his steel-toed work boots. Blood exploded across Clem's lips and cheeks as glass forced itself into the skin around his eyes. He moaned out in pain and rolled onto his back, not sure where the pain was even coming from. Tucker bent forward and tore the revolver loose from Clem's grip, and in an act of frustration and anger brought his boot down, one more time, on Clem's face, nearly caving in his skull and when Tucker saw the outcome of what he did he took off running in the direction of the trailer door.

/ / /

From underneath the trailer Abraham watched as Tucker threw his boot into Clem's face. He took aim with the 9mm, ready to fire off a shot, but was thwarted by a face full of dirt that Finch tossed in his direction. The grit of clay and soil stung his eyes as Finch laid knuckles into his cheekbone, splitting open the skin just below his eye. Abraham slapped at his face to remove the grime and when he could see again, he saw the last glimpse of Finch's feet scampering out from under the trailer.

/ / /

Finch rounded the corner of the burnt-up structure, making his way to its face and to the steps. When he entered, he found Tucker up against a corner looking like a madman ready to be thrown into a padded cell. The inside was charred black from floor to ceiling, pieces of the walls falling away from themselves and letting shafts of light in. What was once a kitchen counter was now seared and splintered, stools turned over on their sides, nothing more than kindling, laid in front of it. On the opposite side of the kitchen area were the remains of a couch, springs poking through blackened cushions. Across from that, a melted TV set looking like a piece of modern art Finch didn't understand, but whose creator would claim it was a comment on modern society. But maybe it was.

Tucker raised the revolver and pointed it at Finch. His hand trembled and Finch noticed. The way he had the shakes, he was liable to pull the trigger even if he didn't mean to.

Finch held up his hands. "Calm down. We don't want to do this here. At least not while one of them could burst through the door at any moment and take us both out."

"The fuck I don't." Tucker wiped snot from under his nose with the sleeve of his jacket. "This whole thing has turned into a mess. I have a girl and a baby to get back to. As far as I'm concerned, I have what I came for." He pushed the gun forward in Finch's direction.

"And how do you propose you get out of here? One of them is still alive—the big one I might add—and he nearly gunned you down out there. I saved your ass, so lower the gun and we'll figure this out." Finch waited a five-count and then said, "We don't have a lot of time. Make your move."

Tucker removed his cap and began running his fingers through his hair, a look of panic on his face. "You know, I appreciate you trying to help me out but I don't need you to save me."

"I didn't make the offer to save you. I did it to save myself." Finch held out his hand in hopes Tucker would hand over the gun.

/ / /

Clem was dead by the time Abraham reached his body. He melted to the ground and rested Clem's misshapen head in his lap, stroking his face. Tears welled up and streamed down his cheeks. He stared into Clem's eyes, now sloping into his skull, and said, "My beautiful boy, I'm sorry. Look what he did to you. This is all my fault. If I could have just been happy with who I am this never would have happened. Instead, I had some idiotic notion that I could be someone else and you had to go and pay the price for my issues. I love you, brother." He ran his palm over Clem's eyes, shutting his eyelids. Then he slid his legs out from under Clem's head and gently rested it on the ground. Abraham stood, a mixed rush of emotion and adrenaline pumping through him like ground glass.

Anger, guilt, sadness. He felt his veins tighten and the weight of the gun in his hand returned. He stepped over Clem's body and called out to Tucker and Finch, "You two are fuckin' dead."

/ / /

Tucker heard the threat. It rose in through the glassless window frame and filled what was at one point a living room. He still hadn't made a decision; take his chances with Finch or go at it with the two-hundred-pound convict whose lover was lying dead just outside the door. A man he had kicked in the face while he was dying. He walked across the floor, the sound of burnt carpet crunching under his boots like Rice Krispies. He kept his arm extended and the gun aimed at Finch as he moved to the window, trying to get a sense of the distance that separated him from Abraham. His mind rolled and rushed. He looked around.

"I'd get away from the window." Finch stepped forward, but the sound of busted glass beneath his sneakers gave him away.

"Stay where you are," Tucker said and looked to either side of the trailer.

"There's no back door if that's what you're looking for. Now, I suggest we come up with a plan. There's only him left and if we're smart about it, we can both leave here with what we want. We take care of the goon outside and go back to the original plan."

"Fuck!" Tucker shouted, knowing that Finch was his only way out. He nodded his head in agreement, his nerves still making him twitch and shake.

"Now lower the gun, please, before you take my head off."

Tucker let his hand fall to his side and as he did, the sound of gunfire erupted from outside, blowing apart the morning. Birds tore ass from a nearby tree and split the sky open in their escape. Finch watched as the bullet entered the side of Tucker's neck and bloodshot the back to mulch. Tucker went down like a sack of feed, coughing, and hissing, blood bubbling from his mouth

Finch sprang from his spot by the kitchen counter and reached Tucker as he hit the floor, and came to rest sprawled out on his back. He writhed on the ground, cupping a hand to the wound. Blood so red that it was nearly black pumped itself through his fingers. The skin on Tucker's face was pulled tight with fear but his eyes were lit with confusion.

"Am I going to die?" He spoke the words through blood.

Finch didn't know how to answer. He looked away, not wanting to keep eye contact out of discomfort, but also not wanting to let this kid see his own fear in his last moments. Finch took Tucker's hand in his own, mustered up the nerve to look into his face, and said, "Yeah, kid, it looks that way. But don't fight it, it'll only make it worse. Just let the warmth wash over you and it'll be over."

"I can't die. I have a baby son. Who's gonna take care of him?" His words were garbled and wet.

"It's alright. Just let go. It'll be alright." Finch kept repeating the words like a mantra—not knowing what else to say—as he held Tucker's hand tighter and thought of the son Tucker spoke of and how he'd be just another casualty of circumstance as a sudden and overwhelming feeling of guilt washed over him because he was doing now for a stranger what he could not for his brother.

Tucker's legs buckled as he struggled to take in one last breath and then his hand went limp in Finch's, and he was gone. What felt like a lifetime was all over in a matter of seconds.

/ / /

Finch took the .38 snub-nosed revolver from Tucker's hand and, keeping low to avoid the same fate, crawled to the window on his stomach. He waited, knowing Abraham would fire off another round. The sound of gunfire filled his ears again and a bullet ripped through the side of the trailer, sprayed Finch with dust and insulation, and took out the remains of an old beer bottle that sat on a corner table. Finch sucked in air, held it in his chest, and lifted himself to peek over the windowsill. He fired through the open window, one...two...three...times, and waited.

All three shots missed their mark and instead ricocheted off some nearby rocks and trees, winding into the morning light with the sound of a door stopper twanging.

Abraham laughed and said, "Looks like you need some practice there, cowboy. Your aim is for shit. Now, if we're done playing O.K. Corral I'd like to come in there and finish this nonsense."

Finch checked the chamber and saw there was one bullet left, reminding him there'd only been four to begin with. He muttered something to himself that even he didn't understand. He wasn't going to be able to hit a moving target nor a still one if he couldn't get a good eye on Abraham's position and he was out ammoed. He scoured the inside of the trailer, his eyes darting back and forth, and then remembered seeing canned food in one of the kitchen cupboards. He stuck the gun in his waistband before crawling back to Tucker's body and unlacing one of his work boots. He removed Tucker's sock, made his way back to the kitchen area, and found the least damaged can that he could find. Finch dropped the slightly blackened can of carrots into the tube sock and wound the slack around his knuckles. He took position near the door trim, his whole body pushed flat against the wall. He waited.

Drops of sweat fell from the tip of his nose. Finch tracked the sound of Abraham's feet moving across the ground as well as his voice, grunting and breathing heavy, anger fueling it all. When Abraham reached the top trailer step, he threw his shoulder into the door and took it right off its hinges, nearly sending himself head over heels across the charred carpet. He turned to see Finch, but it was too late to draw the gun. Finch swung the sock and made contact with Abraham's face, breaking teeth. He reached up to his mouth and his hand came away bloody, a look of stunned confusion painted across his features. Finch swung again, this time aiming for his wrist, and knocked the gun loose. It fell to the floor next to Tucker's body.

Abraham took a stance and threw a punch, but missed Finch by half a foot, still dazed from the hit he took in the face. Finch side stepped Abraham's fist and got behind him, swung the sock a final time, missing his intended mark. The weight of the can instead caused the sock to loop around Abraham's neck, working itself back toward Finch where he caught it and pulled it tight against his throat. Abraham leaned forward in a struggle to get free, but it only caused Finch to pull tighter, choking him out even more and giving the convict the look of a dog being led into a dogfight. After a few moments of struggling with one another, Finch lifted his feet from the ground and hung deadweight, bringing the two of them crashing to the floor.

Two hundred pounds of pure prison muscle knocked the wind from Finch's chest as they both rolled and writhed in pain. Abraham got himself up on one knee, sucking in air, and Finch thought it was over. There was no taking this guy down. But in a split moment, the thought of Maggie and Sarah flashed through his mind, and he found meaning. He threw out his foot and caught Abraham in the face, more teeth breaking under his sneaker. Abraham's legs buckled and he was down on the floor one last time, as Finch rolled over onto his stomach, and using Tucker's body, pulled himself away from Abraham, whose hands were clawing at the air, trying to catch hold of his ankle. Finch pulled himself up from the trailer floor and he stumbled before finding his footing. He jumped Tucker's corpse and hauled ass down the hallway, going so fast that he couldn't stop himself before he crashed through the bathroom door, coming to a halt against the sink, his head breaking the medicine cabinet mirror. For a few brief moments, he reached up to touch his forehead and felt splinters of glass stuck in his skin. Blood ran into his eyes. He caught a glimpse of himself in the cracked mirror, but all he saw was Colm.

Down the hallway came the sound of Abraham getting his footing again. Finch could see him, still dazed, his face bleeding as he reached for the gun that had fallen near Tucker's body. Finch looked at the window and summarized that he wouldn't fit through it, but the floor beneath his feet was thin and burnt, sagging with the weight of himself.

Sandwiched between the sink and the shower stall, Finch leveraged himself with one hand on the sink and the other against the sliding glass door of the shower. He kicked at the floor with both feet, and it fell away in pieces. Finch repeated the process until he got his legs through.

Abraham stormed down the hallway, gun in hand. He fired off one more shot as Finch disappeared through the hole he'd punched out with his feet. The bullet caught Finch in the side as he dropped through the opening and landed on his back with a *thud*. Doing his best to ignore the burning pain at his side where the bullet had torn through the skin, Finch retrieved the revolver from his waistband. He waited with bated breath and when Abraham peered down through the open floor, Finch fired the last round in the chamber.

It entered just below Abraham's chin, taking off the top of his head and throwing bits of brain, blood, and skull along the ceiling. Finch dragged himself out from under the trailer, filled the duffel bag with the money from the buried box, and took off in the direction of the gravel grey Plymouth.

23.

The bullet had only broken skin but judging from the pain emanating from the wound and the amount of blood that had soaked through his shirt, Finch could have sworn he was bleeding to death.

He had pulled the car over half a mile from The Blue Sparrow Inn, figuring it would be a crime scene at that point, and removed his jacket to quickly examine the abrasion on the side of his stomach. He cleaned what blood he could with a handful of fast-food napkins he found in the glove compartment. He needed to get back to his car. He couldn't leave Fulton in the Plymouth. He thought on it and figured his best bet would be to lay low in Dolly's and drink coffee until the coast was clear. Then he'd get in his car and drive as far away from Fulton as he could. When he got to where he was going, he'd see about getting the money to Sarah. He hadn't even counted it. It was a bit, but nowhere near eighty grand.

Still, whatever it was, it would serve the purpose of taking care of his little girl.

Finch dropped the revolver into the duffel bag and buttoned his coat so as to hide the bloody wound as best he could. Then he used the remainder of the napkins to wipe down the steering wheel and dashboard for extra measure. He killed the engine and took the keys from the ignition. Outside the car, he wiped down the door handle, shut it closed with his foot, and walked off in the direction of the diner, the motel, and the two-pump filling station. When he got a ways down the road, he tossed the car keys into the surrounding woods and took his cell phone from his coat pocket. Through a cracked screen the time read 8:04. The state was set to execute his brother in less than twelve hours and Finch just kept walking, still not knowing how he should feel about it, but knowing that either feeling wasn't good.

/ / /

Rawlins paced the parking lot of the gas station, smoking one cigarette after another. After discovering the body of the motel desk clerk, he'd made a call to Greensborough Police Department, knowing he simply didn't have the resources to handle two murder investigations. He then made a second call to Lucinda to inform her of the situation but spared her the details. He let her know that he had no idea when he'd be home. After that, he waited, his stomach in knots, knowing Greensborough media would be descending on the scene like vultures once they caught wind of what had happened. He wouldn't be surprised if they arrived before the extra law enforcement.

He pressed at his abdomen with his fingers, trying to undo the knot that seemed to have formed. Maybe he was developing an ulcer. Yet another thing to add to the already long list of things that getting older entailed. He'd file away the affliction, keeping it next to his bum knee and his hemorrhoids and curse his way through the days as he had been for the last few years.

He burped and tasted acid and metal, then tossed a half-smoked cigarette to the parking lot, telling himself for the thousandth time that it was his last. He walked to the road and looked in the direction of Greensborough, hoping to see a car that would indicate the arrival of a police official. He hated waiting and he was growing more impatient by the minute, dreading the thought of the media showing up first. He didn't want to be the person to have to make the official statement, afraid of what he would look like on TV and in pictures that ran in the newspapers.

He turned his head in the opposite direction, then eyed the motel parking lot across the street hoping to see signs of Tucker, but there was nothing. He'd gotten a few calls from Darlene, but he ignored them, praying she would stay put and do nothing until she got word from him. The whole thing was a mess and the pain in his abdomen was growing worse the longer he thought about the situation and how out of control it had become. Two bodies, a missing brother-in-law, and a career criminal who held Rawlins' fate in his hands. Not to mention, the parked Impala across the street serving as a reminder of it all, as years of bad decision-making seemed to finally be coming down, ready to crush him into oblivion.

As he made his way back to the cruiser something took shape in Rawlins' peripheral, a ghost-like shape that came into focus as he aimed his eyes toward the restaurant across the street, and when his head was fully turned in the object's direction, he was met with the familiar face of Finch McAllister. He moved swiftly across the parking lot of Dolly's and Rawlins watched him move in an almost hurried limp and then disappear inside.

/ / /

Finch hurried across the parking lot; the collar of his coat flipped up to keep the chill of the morning off his neck. The walk from the Plymouth wasn't long, but he was tired and hurting and the low sun kept the Autumn air chilled and crisp. He entered the diner and asked to sit in the back at a booth. Once seated, he ordered coffee. When the waitress left, he stood from the seat and readjusted his coat, then walked off in the direction of the coffee station, telling the waitress who had taken his order that he was just heading to the bathroom.

In the bathroom, he splashed water on his face, then took paper towels from the wall dispenser and stuffed them under his coat to keep the wound covered and the blood from leaking. The events played over in his head. He leaned against a stall and pushed the palms of his hands into his eyes until flecks of white appeared in the black behind his eyelids. He wanted to scream. Not only for himself or Colm, or even Maggie and Sarah but for Mavis and Tucker too. He didn't scream though, instead he swallowed it down like he always did, thinking that maybe Colm had always done the same and that it was years of swallowed grief and pain that finally broke free the night he took the lives of five people.

He threw water on his face one more time and left the bathroom.

When he got back to the table, his coffee was waiting. He dropped the duffel bag at his feet as he slid onto the leather seat, then added cream and sugar to the coffee before taking long slow sips from the steaming mug. He stared out the window. There were a few police cars parked at the gas station, but no ambulances. Either they had already shown up and carted off the bodies, or the police had just arrived and there was a long day of waiting until he could safely return to the Impala. He was starting to see that his initial wrong move had been when he decided to return to Fulton in the first place. The police would want to talk to anyone and everyone that had any connection to the motel in the last few days, and they would only grow more suspicious the longer Finch wasn't showing up. A simple license plate check would give him away and the connection to his brother would only further motivate them to find Finch and haul his ass in. His hands were tied. There was no way around it.

The diner was empty, the only couple in the place having left while Finch was in the bathroom. There was an eerie sort of quiet that filled the place, with the occasional clank of dishes and silverware coming from the kitchen staff in the back. He took out his cell phone and placed it on the table beside his mug. He stared at it for a while, contemplating calling Maggie to explain the situation. Tell her to come get the money and that no matter what happened to him afterward, to never speak a word about it.

The entrance bell rang, and Finch looked up from his phone. His first glimpse of the man didn't register at first, but as he got closer to the table, Finch noticed that he walked with a limp, and he knew then that it was Sheriff Lou Rawlins. The keys that hung from his belt jangled as he approached the booth. His spit-shined shoes clacked against the checkered floor. The sound was like pins in Finch's brain.

He called out to the waitress who was turning to greet the cop. "Miss, can I get another cup of coffee?" Finch held up the mug.

She told Rawlins to sit anywhere he liked as she carried a fresh pot of coffee to Finch's table and poured him a cup. Rawlins slid into the seat across from Finch, then looked up at the waitress.

"When I said 'anywhere', Sheriff, I didn't mean tables that were already occupied." She giggled a nervous laugh at her comment.

"It's fine," Finch said. "Sort of been waiting for him to show up sooner or later."

She looked at Finch, a curious look on her face, not quite understanding what he meant by the comment. She shrugged it off, looked down at Rawlins, and asked, "Would you like anything?"

"No thank you, but in all seriousness, this man is a suspect in the crimes that took place next door and across the street, so it would probably be best for you and anyone else in the back to mosey on out of here. He could be armed, and I don't need any more trouble today."

She thought he was joking at first, but quickly realized he wasn't when the muscles in his face didn't move an inch.

She turned her head toward Finch, who didn't take his eyes off Rawlins. "Best to do what he says, Ma'am," he said, not wanting any more people dead. There just wasn't any way to know how this was going to play out.

The waitress set the coffee pot down on the counter. She went into the back and after a few moments, she and two other men appeared. Finch assumed it was probably the cook and the dishwasher. The man with the grease-stained apron asked if everything was alright and Rawlins told him what he'd told the waitress. The three of them left through the front door, leaving Finch alone with the Sheriff.

Finch looked out the window as he spoke. "Don't you have some more important work to tend to across the street, Louis?"

Rawlins grimaced. He hated it when anyone aside from his mother called him that. He felt his blood pressure rise. "This has been a long time coming,"

Rawlins said and leaned into the table. "Now, where is it?" He spoke the words through clenched teeth.

"Is that seriously all you care about? Don't you want to know about the kid you sent to do your dirty work since you aren't man enough to do it yourself?"

"Where is it?"

"Another kid whose life was snuffed out due to your incompetence. How many people's lives are on your hands, Sheriff?" Finch turned his head away from the window and met Rawlins' gaze.

"Where the fuck is my father's gun, Finch. That's the last time I'm asking."

Finch kicked the bag at their feet.

Rawlins leaned away from the table and peered down at the duffel bag, and then leaning back in his seat he said, "We're not a passive breed, Finch. The whole human race denounces violence from the safety of their living rooms, but our history shows us something different. So, answer me this, which one is lying? Point being, corral enough people and get them riled up and all sorts of morals fall away."

"Where is this coming from?"

"Fucked if I know. Thinking out loud, I suppose. Trying to justify my actions."

"You're not doing a very good job of it."

Rawlins looked up from a spot on the table where his eyes had been glued. "Do you think you're better than me? You can sit there and smirk and say that I shot an innocent man based on what you think is racially motivated, but you don't know the full story. And worst of all, for three years you've held in your possession the one thing that could have given his death justice. But you don't care about that. You've chosen to use it for your own selfishness. To gain the upper hand. So don't sit there and think you're any different than me. We're more alike than you care to admit. We're hypocrites and cheaters and, even worse, liars."

"I'm a liar now too?"

"Do you know what the definition of a lie is? A lie isn't only giving a false answer when asked a question, but also denying others of the knowledge to which they are entitled. So yeah, you're a liar."

"Even if that's the case, how is that worse than being a murderer?"

"You're only proving my point. We all make excuses for our bad behavior, no matter how small, telling ourselves it's not as bad as the next person's sins because we've all convinced ourselves that it's different when we do it. Your brother slaughters an entire family, and you go to bat for him but condemn me while holding onto evidence just to keep your own ass out of prison for crimes you've committed. I may have taken a life and ruined more in the process, but you've been stopping a family from getting closure. I caused the wound, but you refuse to heal it."

"I never went to bat for my brother. Never tried to make excuses for what he did. All I've done is try to understand why."

"And?"

"It's not something I care to share with you at the present moment."

"I'm offended. I thought we were friends. The things we've been through together," Rawlins leaned into the table and whispered, "The secrets we share." He took a pack of cigarettes from his pocket and lit one. He squinted through the smoke trailing off the cherry.

"Can I get one of those?" Finch reached under his coat and felt the wound and winced, the skin around the rupture feeling as soft and wet as an over-ripened plum. His hand came out bloody and Rawlins slid the pack of cigarettes across the table. Finch took one, stuck it in his mouth, and said, "Light?"

Rawlins retrieved a disposable lighter from his shirt pocket and handed it to Finch. He lit it, set the lighter on the table, and took long, slow drags, savoring every inhale. "My first cigarette in three years," Finch said, resting it between two bloody fingers.

"And what's the verdict?"

"As beautiful as I remember."

There was a moment of silence that seemed to stretch on forever as the two men sat across from one another smoking their cigarettes.

Rawlins eased back against the seat. "You ever have to clean the shit from your own mother's ass? You ever had to look your mother in the eyes knowing full well those are the same eyes you've known and memorized since you were dick high and see no recognition as she stares back at you? Like she's staring at a stranger. The man she gave birth to. And the longer you stare the more you think it'll finally dawn on her and she'll finally find you, but that moment is rare and getting rarer by the day, and when it does happen, it lasts a mere few minutes. Not enough time to relive a memory together and share a laugh or even say I love you without it all going to waste. Have you ever had to bathe her? Something no child should have to do for their parent. An eighty-year-old woman reduced to nothing more than a husk, a caricature of her former self, living on a steady diet of fuckin' baby food that's shoveled into her mouth by a spoon. Waking up at all hours of the night, screaming her husband's name, wondering where she is and where he is and why he isn't in bed next to her. Having to explain to her that he's been dead for twenty years. You give up after the first thousand times, really, because you can't bear to watch her relive all that grief over again like she hadn't already been through it and moved on. People tell you to put her in a home, that she'll be taken care of, but you know you can't do that. You know those places are not where anyone should be in their final moments, so you take care of her like she took care of you because you can't bear to get a phone call telling you she's gone and having to live with the regret of not having been with her when she finally slipped off. Everyone is dealt a hand and the only thing you can do is find a way to play that hand the best you can. So yeah, I've done things I'm not proud of. And regardless of what you or anyone else thinks, I'm not gonna throw away a fuckin' twenty-year career so my mother can sit and rot and die in some home run by people who don't care about anything but collecting a paycheck. It all boils down to the safety and comfortability of my family, which easily outweighs any morals I may have. Same as you. Same as Tucker."

"You're fuckin' psychotic, you know that?"

"Again, a psychotic is someone with a skewed view of reality, which is what *you* are if you think this thing plays out any way that doesn't end with your death."

Finch raised his eyes toward Rawlins but kept his head pointed down at the table. Rawlins was right. Finch knew exactly how it was going to play out, and at that moment, he didn't even feel inclined to fight it. Finch's line of thinking had always been like a fault line, and he'd spent the better part of his life living through the thoughts, always hoping he'd be able to survive the inevitable. He'd arrived. And along with the threat of death came half-muted whispers, dark voices that were darker than anything that had come before them, turning a slightly lesser shade of night as they made their way through his skull and toward his frontal lobe, like skipping stones across a pond.

"This is me letting you know that I have my gun pointed at you from under this table," Rawlins said. "Don't feel bad though. There will always be debts owed. We all pay a price for the things we do and the things we don't do. The only option is to pick which poison you prefer, suck it back in silence, and await the consequence. It's just not my turn yet."

Finch blinked slowly, his eyelids feeling like they weighed fifty pounds each. He dropped the cigarette in his coffee cup. It sizzled. Outside, state police had begun showing up. Rawlins watched over his shoulder as they pulled their cars into the parking lot of the gas station.

"I suppose that's my cue to mosey on out of here," Rawlins said. He turned his head away from the window and looked at Finch.

"I suppose so."

"Any chance you wanna enlighten me with what the hell went on last night?"

"I don't reckon I do."

"I didn't think you would," Rawlins said, and then his chest heaved slightly with a laugh.

"What's funny?" Finch asked.

"I'm just thinking about how your brother has spent the last five years of his life on death row, is scheduled to be executed tonight, and he's still gonna outlive you. Life sure has weird ways of working itself out."

They met each other's gaze and Finch heard one last whisper from the dark, *Sometimes love turns violent*," and then he closed his eyes and thought of Sarah as Rawlins fired two shots into his stomach from under the table.

Finch spasmed, one…two…three times, then felt his muscles tighten as blood worked its way up into his throat where it puddled halfway then slid from his mouth in slow but thick streams. Rawlins watched it all from across the table, wishing Finch would die quicker so he could get on with his day. And just when Rawlins thought he was going to have to screw a bullet into Finch's skull, it happened. Finch went limp and his upper half slumped over the tabletop, knocking over the coffee cup and spilling it to the floor. The bullet wounds hissed and spit blood. Rawlins heard them gurgle from where he sat. He looked down at Finch and took note of the smile stretched across the now corpse's pale, lifeless face. He stood from the booth, whistling as he did, took the duffel bag from the floor, and walked out of the diner and into the morning sun which hung in the endless cobalt blue sky above. And as he eyed the sky stretching toward Greensborough and beyond, Rawlins wondered what the hell a dead man had to smile about.

ACKNOWLEDGMENTS

The author wishes to thank the following people for whom the writing of this book would have not been possible: **India LaPlace**, for giving me the much-needed space and time it takes to write a novel in the first place, and for being the first to read it and give me feedback even if I didn't want to listen at first. I love you. **Michael Nau**, for taking the time to read through the first draft and giving me critiques, and pointing out the areas where I fail as a writer. You're a good man to have on my side. **Melissa Koehler** for the continuing support despite everything else. You're still one of my favorite people. And finally, **Everyone** who has ever bought one of my previous books. Even though it all seems pointless a lot of the time it's you that makes it worth it. There is a debt that is owed to all mentioned that could never be paid. Thank you.

Philip LoPresti is an author and photographer living in Upstate New York. His photography can be found at philiplopresti.com or on his Instagram. When he's not writing he can be found watching horror, western, and crime films.

www.ingramcontent.com/pod-product-compliance
Lightning Source LLC
Chambersburg PA
CBHW022034240626
47154CB00007B/2401